The Maid of Flowerdale

Night Court of Wolfstone: Act I

© Tom Oden Ahlqvist 2019
Publisher: Books on Demand, Stockholm, Sweden
Print: Books on Demand, Norderstedt, Germany
Maps and dwellings: Tom Oden Ahlqvist
Book Cover and border: Nomi Bontegard
Brigand Camp: Jonas Gustavsson
ISBN: 978-91-7851-044-3

Table of Contents

The Maid of Flowerdale

The soft and warm spring winds were rustling the leaves of the calm and lush woodlands of Coille a Deas, the southernmost part of the great Wayland forest, bordering both Huntsfirth and Usentil in the north. Miranda Belltower, youngest daughter of the nearby town's reeve, was on her way home after having gathered wild berries for the length of the afternoon. She was weary but blissful, her eyes sparkling with joy. Her marriage was drawing nearer each day, oh how she looked forward to it! To think that her prayers to Nidesfarn, Father of the Gods, became answered! That she and the handsome, confident son of the baron of the lands fell for each other, even though she was a mere town-reeve's daughter. And the youngest, no less. Her steps were light upon the small forest path, and often she danced a few steps forward. Her long, black hair was knotted into a braid, so she wouldn't get caught in twigs and branches, but she did wear a double layered dress of linen covered with wool. It was bright green, as the local fashion had been for, well as far back as she'd heard. After all, she and the people of Faerann Eadar were Alerians, and had always been fond of woodland colours. Now leaves and spring flowers were blooming, and her dress matched the innocence and youth they showed quite strikingly.

Walking down from the woods into Flowerdale, the town she had lived in for all her life, was as enjoyable as ever. The townsfolk were going about their business, merchants were about to start packing their unsold wares, young children were running around, either playing with each other, or trying to collect their hens and chickens for the night. They had lost quite a few over the years to foxes, and one or two goblins. Her thoughts strayed away for a moment to the evil creatures of the world. She thought about the men and women currently stationed in the Harg Mountains, a long way to the south, well past the Highland Heads, who had to fight the blackbloods night and day. How thankful she was that she lived in the northern kingdom, far away from strife and woes. And more thankful yet, that nobles were always given positions of high ranks in the armies. Her beloved would not have to expose himself for, well at least as much danger as the soldiers of the Hunter Banners. She shuddered at her dark thoughts and shook them out of her head. On her way to the town hall, she greeted and was greeted by many of the townsfolk. She was very fond of them, and they of her, as she was a kind and good-hearted girl. Even though she had a higher station then the commoners, she never made it apparent, and in fact felt out of place every time she had to attend meetings at the baron's estate. Or worse still, attending the court at Caislean Uisce, when matters of importance to the whole county needed deliberating.

She opened the door to her family home next to the town hall. It was twice as large as those of ordinary merchants, attendants, serfs and craftsmen, but she thought nothing of it. After all, the administration of the town and its nearby farms was a burden of responsibility, and personal space was a just reward for carrying it. Miranda rounded a wall at the far end of the hall and greeted her father, Town-reeve Thomir Belltower. He sat in his study, writing numbers on papers. God, if he did anything else on his spare time! she thought and gave him a fond smile.

"Counting food supplies for Lordanan are we?" she asked teasingly. Her father looked up, a sincere look on his face.

"His name will be *Count Ainsley* henceforth young woman. How many times have I told you this?" he asked and smiled back, not too resolute in seeing his words lived up to.

"As many times as to this day, but a hundred times that and more still!" she proclaimed, and kissed her father on his bald scalp. He turned to face her and stroke her arm lovingly.

"What would Tearlach think once you two are married, and you forget his lord's title? These things are very important to all the peers of the realm you know."

Miranda's thoughts went to her beloved in an instant. Yes, he would surely live up to customary respect, both deserved and that earned by lineage. But she would remember how to behave at the court. As Tearlach was the only heir to Brodan and Eileen Cairlin, Lord and Lady of the land, she would become the future baroness. She thought about walking around in the estate garden, such a delightful and tranquil place! She thought about going on hunts with Tearlach, and dining with him at the grand banquet hall in the estate. She delighted in the fact that the Cairlins choose the etiquette that lord's and lady's chairs were placed at each other's side, and not in opposite ends of the long table, as was the other option for nobles in the three kingdoms of Broadland.

On the way to her private chambers, she peeked into her sister's room. The older sibling was not there, and had not been seen much as of late. She wondered why, and dwelt on why Liara had been in such a foul mood lately. She hardly ate anything, and frequently frowned at things Miranda said. She felt sorry for her sister, and wished that she too would be blessed by Nidesfarn, so that she could feel just as happy as she herself did in this moment. She put the baskets full of berries on a table. Wearily, she let herself fall down onto the soft goose-feather bed, and with all clothes still on, she fell into blissful sleep.

Setting up the Game

Flowerdale is meant to be played by 2-4 players and a Game Master (henceforth known as GM). Its main story is a murder mystery, and the mood you want to portray is the stark contrast between the beautiful and peaceful region and the horrific crime that has been committed there. As the players continue to delve deeper into the murder case, they will uncover dark forces lurking beneath the layers of everyday life the region is accustomed to. What the players choose to do will result in different consequences and endings, and the GM must refrain from choosing sides. The adventure is set in the world of Vindeon, and uses the rules provided in the main lore and rules book by the same name.

It is important that you, the GM, are well prepared before each game session, and it is the goal of this adventure book to provide you with the means to be so.

Before you can begin this adventure, you need the following:
- *Vindeon – An Adventure Role-playing Game.* This adventure's Core Rulebook.
- A set of role-playing dice containing at least one of each of the following: d4, d6, d8, d10, d12, d20. Preferably more.
- Vindeon Character Sheets (Included in the Vindeon Core Rulebook)
- Pencils and scribbling papers

An important tip for you in your role as the GM is to create a few *Encounters* and *Side Quests* as the adventures progresses. They usually create flavour and everything from weird to epic situations. In the best of worlds, your players create these situations themselves, but if they lack the energy, experience or are too focused on the main quest, you need to step in to create diversions. Vindeon is full of monsters and forgotten places, as well as colourful characters in every town, hamlet and castle.

The main theme of this adventure is mystery solving, and therefore, it contains lots of conversations, reactions between non-player characters and counter-reactions, as well as hidden or inaccessible places which the players must find a way to explore. This also means that the adventure does not contain a lot of combat encounters. If you know your group likes fast action and dice rolls, to put their characters in mortal danger, you should consider adding a few combat encounters or even side quests.

Chapter Overview

The Maid of Flowerdale
Flavour text, meant to be read out loud once you are set and ready to begin the adventure.

True Events and Motives
Explains the main plot, what has happened and why, and so, you can safely say that it is what actually happened. The plot chapter contains major spoilers and should be kept secret by the GM. Players will unlock more parts of the plot as their adventure progresses. This chapter also contains short insights in alerian culture and societal structures, to give the GM a picture of the people in whose lands the adventure takes place. *Alerian* is an ancient collective term for the language, culture, faith and people who live in the three realms of Broadland.

The Investigation by Player Progression
This chapter is the main storyline of the adventure. It describes in general terms how the adventure starts and what can happen, depending on how good the players are at accumulating evidence and outmanoeuvring the evil characters. It has three milestones: the beginning, the first court and the second court. The adventure is split into two acts. Act I ends before the first court, at a secret meeting with Tearlach. Depending on how well they did, the players may unlock different parts of the Cairlin Estate and gain more allies. Act II begins with the first court and ends with the final court, where some characters will be found guilty and others innocent. The second court is also the end of the adventure.

Main Characters, Supporting Characters, Other NPC's
These chapters contain a list of the more important characters in the adventure, their personalities, backstories and suggestions of how the GM should play them. Important to note is that it is here the GM finds information about what the different characters know about the happenings, and also how they react if confronted by the players with proofs, accusations, or requests for aid in solving the murder mystery. Where they are found in the world is also described.

Supporting characters are presented next. They have limited background and impact on the adventure as a whole, but are still important as they support the main characters and players may unlock new areas, possibilities and conversations through them. Lastly, a number of other NPC's (Non-Player Characters, played out by the GM) are listed such as guards, monsters and vendors.

Maps and Places
This chapter contains three maps: The first one a map of the entirety of Broadland and its three realms: The Crown of Noralac, the Midland Realm and the Crown of Cathalon. The second map zooms in on the Duchy of Loingseach, southwestern Noralac, to provide GM and players with an orientation to surrounding areas. The last map is zoomed in on the Faerann Eadar county, southern Loingseach, where the adventure takes place. This is the map in play. All its points of interest, such as towns, castles, forests and mountains are presented, leaving only farms, fields and some streams to your own imagination.

Places of importance to the plot will be more thoroughly described, providing GM with flair and useful information about them, for example if a *Character* resides at the place, or where items can be found. Gaining access to certain levels and areas of estates and other places can be done by either player dialogue with non-playable characters (NPC's) to unlock via story progression, by successful skill rolls, or exploration.

True Events and Motives

In 9010, Lord Tearlach Cairlin was born, first son of House Cairlin. He was born of Baroness Eileen Cairlin, Baron Brodan's wife. He was raised like all other noble sons of the realm; spending much time with his father learning how to fight, how to command and how to rule the lands his family owned by blood and acceptance from the Northern Crown. At age twenty-two, he first laid his eyes on Miranda Belltower, the daughter of the reeve of Flowerdale, the main settlement in the land governed by his father, and fell in love with her. As it so happened, he was a young man of incredible willpower, and it was firmly believed by most he would far surpass his father as a baron. And so, even though his parents had the rights to pair him with a woman of similar station and renown, everyone knew he would merely wait until he had gathered enough reasons to enact divorce by law, either by violating the sacred bonds himself, or driving his wife to do likewise. Brodan and Eileen Cairlin knew this, and even though Eileen despised this fact, her force of will similar to young Tearlach, she knew she would not be able to influence him to marry a lady of her choice.

Sometimes a match between man and woman seems so perfect most people can only explain it as fate or the act of higher entities. This was the fact with Tearlach and Miranda. Their love to each other obvious, they completed one another in many ways. Tearlach was confident and brave, Miranda positive and empathic, both loving. On his twenty-third birthday, he proclaimed she would be the girl he would wed. Even though it was nothing short of a cultural crime to decline the proposals of nobles of higher station, men and women could, theoretically, decline a noble's proposal. Needles to say, Miranda did not.

However, there were individuals disappointed with this loving young couple's union. In fact, the county of Faerann Eadar contained more than a few lords and ladies. There was the knightly family of Rock of Dien to the north, with their three daughters, waiting for an opportunity to increase their standing within the county by marrying into a lineage governing land. As a knightly family they had a high standing within the alerian military, but lacked civil renown. On the western shores of the county a great estate tower in the distance, clearly visible from their main town Murchaddan. It houses the second barony of Faerann Eadar, first if comparing influence; House Tuil. Worse still was that they controlled incoming and outgoing sea trade to the west and was thus unequally rich in comparison to all other lords and ladies of the land, save Count Lordanan the Seafarer who owned the county. House Tuil had four daughters, all of them fair and compassionate. And expensively dressed. The Cairlin barony had no port, overshadowed by the awe inspiring Caislean Uisce – home of Count Lordanan. The castle was built upon a natural rock out in the water, behind it a deep-water bay, perfect for docking heavy ships. Subsequently, the castle was built upon the rock and a port town emerged quickly beneath its protecting walls. The easternmost tower became a beacon to guide vessels into the port, and the whole setup quickly became famous throughout Loingseach, connecting to all other major ports of Broadland around Grimlake, among them Fidh and Cathalon, home to the rulers of two of the three alerian realms.

All this, Baroness Eileen Cairlin considered whilst stalking back and forth through the halls of her estate. Her son was a fool! Marrying the stupid daughter of a mewling little town reeve too unimportant to be recognized even by the officials of Uisce Port! She thought about her dark past and the shadows swirled within, fuelled by her displeasure. Shortly after the birth of her son she was forced to travel through Wayland Forest - a menacing woodland separating Broadland and Rhuedi, because her brother had met his end under mysterious circumstances there. She was bound to attend his funeral, but soon found herself in the claws of a greater vampire - Count Iorval Wolfstone. He took her into his undying embrace, teeth sunk into artery, and the baroness became immortal. She found strength in the darkness, and Count Wolfstone sensed it. Knowing he had gained a powerful ally, he let her go back to her earlier life, bound to slowly corrupt and twist Faerann Eadar, setting yet another part of Broadland on the path to eternal damnation. Because of the undying curse, she could not conceive again, making young little Tearlach all the more precious to her. Shortly after her return, Baron Brodan fell to the ruinous powers of darkness as well. Over the course of Tearlach's childhood, the estate slowly turned sinister and foreboding. The colours of the once red and green banners of the house turned dark and pale, and the expressions of their ancestor's faces on the wall paintings seemed more sinister for each passing year. More and more windows were shut, but the Cairlins never made it nearly obvious enough that something was wrong to the outside world. On the banquets, everything was polished, windows opened to let fresh air in from Grimlake, music played loud and merry, much like the talk of the houseguests.

But there were strange disappearances. Mostly women, but men alike, vanished in the woods of the region. There was talk about trolls and goblins, but whispers arose about one or more witches prowling the forest paths in search of prey. Since the disappearances were far and few between, the rumours never really took hold, especially not in the good town

of Flowerdale. In truth however, Lady Cairlin was the instigator of the rumours, for in fact, it was she and her husband who abducted the victims in the woods during foggy, moonless nights. They took great care not to bereft any locals of their freedom – they did not want any witch hunts to commence, for the simple fact that there were no witches prowling the woods. Dungeons beneath the estate were built in secrecy, only accessible via a trapdoor behind the bookshelf in the master bedroom, as well as from a nondescript barn in the outskirts of the estate grounds. There, the poor victims were drained of blood, and no one ever escaped to tell the horrid tale. If suspicions grew too large, which had happened a few times, the Cairlins simply framed some unimportant person, preferably one living by themselves away from the villages and farmsteads, soon thereafter accusing them of witchcraft. When the first witch was taken into custody, the Cairlins officially built a smaller dungeon in the basement were they would await their trial. Town officials rarely gained audience with these supposed "witches", and frankly, little did they care, as they wanted as little to do with the dark influence they wrought as possible. After all, the alerian belief in the spirits was a faith balancing between light and darkness, and it was common for fogwalkers, as the spiritual leaders of their people were called, to sooner or later succumb to the darkness of evil spirits or human desire and vanity. Too common in fact, which was part of the reason why many Alerians looked towards their eastern neighbours and their peaceful Sigan faith in which the spiritworld was left to the dead alone. Thus, the Cairlin vampires had a perfect setup for themselves. As long as they continued to be careful they would have a steady stream of blood from their victims, both the "real ones" and those accused of witchcraft. Torture was the preferred way of dealing with witches, as Alerians deemed it fair punishment for the pain inflicted by them upon others. As young Tearlach grew older, he came to fully realize what was being done to the poor wretches. He alone was allowed, or rather not stopped, to converse with the witches. They did not seem wicked or evil to him, and often, his heart was torn by their cries and seemingly innocent anguish. He could not stand to watch the executions until several years of being forced to do so. But it strengthened him. Made him accustomed to pain and death. His feelings encased in a shell of ice, there was only force of will and a sense of what's good that prevented him from falling into despair. For naught could he do to stop the punishments. Such were the laws.

His frozen heart did at last thaw as it was put close to the loving heart of Miranda, and once more, his righteousness welled within him. Once marriage was complete, he would stop this foul exercise at his estate once and for all.

~¤~

Liara was the older daughter of Thomir Belltower and she adored Tearlach just as much as her sister, maybe even more. Her heart shattered completely by the fact made clear that the handsome, caring young lord fell completely before the beauty and charms of her younger sister Miranda. Alas, poor Liara! Her soul wailed, her desire longing for his arms and his love. She fell into despair. Lost appetite and paled considerably. Dark rings entrenched themselves around her green eyes like a besieging army a walled town. Her only comfort was away from people, away from her father. And especially, away from her sister, which she both loved and hated at the same time. Anything would have been better than this! She would even be happier if he were to marry one of the other ladies of the lands. One that was of higher ranking than she and her sister. At least that would have felt better, knowing Tearlach probably would have wed one of them out of political necessity rather than that wondrous feeling called love.

Sitting on a mossy log one day brooding, she was greeted by the Baroness.

It took some convincing recruiting Liara to her scheme, but ultimately Liara agreed. Eileen had procured a sleeping poison from one of her northern contacts and had consequently offered it to Liara. It was supposed to last for seven weeks and would make Miranda seem dead, her heartbeats undetectable but still faint, keeping her at the border between the spiritworld and the physical world, never really crossing over. She would be dead and mourned by Tearlach and buried for all to bear witness. The marriage would be cancelled, presenting a perfect opportunity for the jealous sister to mend the young lord's wounds, embrace him in her arms, and make him realize how she bore the same attributes as her sister, and hopefully, gained feelings for her. Once Miranda awoke, the Baroness had promised to extract her from the realms. She was to be moved to the harsh fjord gards of the vorgar in the north-eastern reaches of the world. Eileen promised Liara her sister would be presented as a chamber maid of House Cairlin, and that she would retain the same station in Vorgland. Liara did not agree instantly. Instead, she brooded and deliberated. Her love for her sister was indeed strong, but as the Baroness' promise sank deeper into her mind, and as the time of marriage drew nearer, she agreed to enact poisoner. The plan was easy: Liara would poison her sister and put the blame on a young girl, most obviously a witch, who emerged at Whitebay and tried to ensnare them both with occult sorcery. Miranda had acted out of love and heroically thrust herself forward towards the witch, taking the full force of the sinister spell. The witch had been hit by her lifeless body, felled to the ground by the sheer momentum Miranda had attained. Liara would then have enraged, and attacked the defenceless witch. A fight supposedly occurred, where Liara was able to rip off a tuft of the witch's blonde hair and also her plain copper necklace meagrely adorned by a simple rose-quartz stone before she, still quite formidable, had been able to free herself to flee into the forest, her attempt obviously half failed. Meanwhile, the Baroness "liberated" one of her house servants of just such a tuft of hair and her plain copper necklace was stolen. Not that any one cared, but her name was Ellen, picked from one of Usentil's many orphanages on her seventh birthday. Now she was fifteen. Wicked Eileen was to give the tuft to Liara who could then frame and accuse Ellen of being the witch, in turn unleashing the full wrath of the family members of House Cairlin upon the poor girl. Well, almost everyone. Tearlach would probably be difficult. On the other hand, Baroness Cairlin was very certain of her scheme.

~¤~

Five days prior to the wedding, Liara nervously approached Miranda, trying to appear sincere, and asked her out for a walk along the sandy beach of Whitebay - an area of the eastern coast formed as an almost full lagoon of shallow water, as they had for so many times before. Miranda lit up in a warm smile, hopeful that her sister had come to terms with the fate bestowed upon them both. Little did she know what lay ahead.

Upon reaching the beautiful beach, her sister assaulted her, quickly forcing the contents of the small vial down her throat before she realized what was happening. Liara held her sister as she saw the life in her eyes flicker and die. Her eyelids closed, a last sigh escaped from her lungs, and her body slumped in Liaras embrace. Panic struck her that instant, as she realized what she had done, the irreversibility of her crime and the unfathomable suffering she had inflicted on her own sister. She realized then what the feeling of guilt meant. Of sincere regret. She slumped down with her sister still in her arms, cried and lamented her evil deed. Eyes swollen and tear-stricken, she asked first her sister for forgiveness, then the spirits. In that moment, Mirandas body quivered, and became still as a rock. Liara stopped crying, an even greater fear widening her eyes in true terror. Carefully, she leaned over her sister and put an ear to her mouth. Nothing. Shaking of dread, she pressed her ear to Miranda's chest, to her heart. She was promised by the Baroness that she would be able, if she waited for at least a hundred of her own heartbeats, to feel a very faint heartbeat. She waited and waited. A hundred of her fast pacing, pounding heartbeats passed. A hundred more, and a hundred more. After that, it dawned on her. Miranda had entered the eternal sleep. Her future was never to be seen, her love for Tearlach never to bloom. In her most joyous of days, on a warm, sunbathed beach glittering of a thousand little sand grains, Miranda lay still.

Liara's raving thoughts attacked her from all angles in all forms. She was all but lost in a state of lethargy when survival kicked in. It forced her up on her feet. Its cold logic told her it was over for Miranda, nothing would ever change that, but she could still improve her own situation. Lessen her distress. She remembered the plan and promptly made it towards the secret barn leading into the dungeons of the Cairlin estate, where Eileen awaited with Ellen's belongings.

The old and cunning vampire inspected the broken girl standing, panting, before her. A sorry sight indeed. Weak. Weakness disgusted Eileen almost as much as low born humans. Liara fit both descriptions. She saw what she had foreseen; the girl would not be able to bear the burden of guilt in her current state. She would confess, putting the baroness herself in a less than preferable position. And so, she proceeded as she had planned all along. She conjured an enslavement spell of immense potency, her ordinary way of pinning victims down. Shackles of pure energy wrapped themselves around Liara's hands and feet, and she could do nothing but stare in horror, as the betrayer neared her. She saw the features of the Baroness pale, and how a wicked grin revealed a sinister truth – a truth no man or woman in the whole duchy knew. Excitement rushed through the crooked vampire, as she gave Liara the kiss of death - the first part in the spell which turned a human into undead vampire. And then, she grabbed Liara's hair and yanked her head back, exposing her large veins on her neck, bulging from stress. There was no need for tenderness. She sunk her canines straight into Liara's left artery, bypassing the clearly visible veins. As the tips of teeth penetrated the artery walls, unholy magic coursed from them into the hapless victim, replacing the rejuvenating, steaming blood that was flowing into Eileen. When the vampire was sated, Liara's soul was shackled, much like her body, in eternal damnation and undeath. By turning Liara into a vampire, not only had she secured a calm and cold-hearted witness to the made-up witch attack, she had also gained an eternal servant - a maiden of perpetual night. With a sinister grin, Eileen beheld the transformation. Once completed, she cast a blood surge spell on the poor girl, a spell which forced capillaries to burst and blood to flow out from eyes, ears and mouth, just to make it even more believable that the two sisters were victims of a witch's assault. Confused and drained, broken Liara arose to receive the blonde tuft of hair, and the copper necklace.

The Investigation by Player Progression

The news of Miranda's death devastated young Tearlach, but if ever he had shown traits of extreme determination, it was now. He immediately set off for Whitebay to search for the body of Miranda. It was not there, but clearly, there had been some commotion. He desperately wanted to jump off his horse and commence a search for her, but realized he was needed at the estate to hinder rash decisions at court by his parents or Miranda's father, who was surely as woeful as he.

In the meantime, Eileen sent out the estate guards to look for the body, but they were unable to locate it, as it seemed to have vanished. They went out to the beach and forest paths in two shifts, the first ones returning fruitless just before dusk, the other searching without success in the night, making it almost impossible to distinguish trails due to the poor light provided by torches.

The remainder of that day and the following night, between his fits of exhaustion due to grief, Tearlach focused all his attention into the investigation of the murder of his beloved and betrothed. It seemed all too suspicious that Miranda would happen to get killed by a mad witch, the only witness being her own sister, which in turn managed to survive by luck, even succeeding in chasing the witch away, tearing loose some hair and a copper necklace, undoubtingly pointing to one of his family's own house maids. Ellen was her name, it seemed, and the few times he had noticed her, she seemed to him an ordinary girl, rather good and empathic. By the aid of recognition by his parents, Miranda's sister had presented the evidence to her father, Thomir, who in his unfathomable grief had demanded the immediate execution of said girl, after the trial was held at the Cairlin Court. Hate and grief burned in the eyes of the otherwise loveable and peaceful town reeve. Tearlach knew time was of the essence as the manorial court consisting of his two parents, Town Reeve Thomir Belltower and the three First Leaders John Wood, Ida Hayleah and Bordrin Somersburn, would surely deem the girl guilty as charged. The only thing he could do was to act as the girl's defender, and demand the matter be investigated further by higher authority, or more exactly, Nathair Falconer – *Lord Captain* (Law Enforcement Commander) of Faerann Eadar and Count Lordanan the Seafarer's second in command. The Lord Captain was the only one who needed some time to arrive as he was stationed in Uisce Port about four seven kilometres to the south of Flowerdale. Additionally, the Lord Captain had more important business to attend to. Less than interested, he was scheduled to arrive in two days.

Tearlach thus had two days to make his own investigation. Too little time to make a complete one by himself. He needed to hire private investigators. People that did not have any ties to this region at all, for he could not know what alliances and pacts had been made by whom behind closed doors. They did not need to be master reeves or guard captains. He was of a mind that the more diverse his private investigators were, the higher the chance would be that they managed to find out as much as possible, as different skills could reveal different clues. He did the only thing he could do, even though it would cause some stir and unwanted attention. He went down to Flowerdale's market row, and started talking with the strangers and travellers there, ending his recruitment run at the local inn: "The Hare & Pheasant".

It is in these two places he finds and hopefully recruits the Player Characters. This is how the adventure starts. As reward, he offers each one ten gold coins and a Raven Duty emblem – a reward given by alerian nobles to persons that has proven themselves worthy of their lord's gratitude by sword, word or work. Often in combination.

Act I – Detective work

The first act starts when one or more players are about to enter an inn after sunset when five dark outriders (the second search party of Eileen's) blast through the town in full dash. It seems they are in a great hurry.

Act I is all about finding clues and leads, talking to different characters, visiting and investigating different places. Tearlach wants to know what happened to Miranda and find her body. They have two days to complete their investigation. On the third day, the first court is held. Judges are Nathair Falconer, Thomir Belltower, Eileen and Brodan Cairlin, John Wood, Ida Hayleah and Bordrin Somersburn. Liara Belltower stands as witness to the murder, and Ellen the Housemaid is the accused. Tearlach Cairlin acts as her defender. Act I ends just before the first trial.

In Act I, there are five different points of interest as to how Miranda died: *Whitebay, Mordoc's "Fishing" Shack, Troll Cave, Brigand Camp* and *Secret Barn Entrance*.

Whitebay is the obvious starting place for the investigation as it is the actual crime scene. The players will hopefully detect a small fishing shack built on the south edge of the bay where the jagged coastal rocks begin to form. That is *Mordoc's "Fishing" Shack*. A necromancer lives there and he retrieved the body of Miranda and kept it in his basement. If they succeed in getting some information out of him, he will reveal his "medical" examination results are not pointing towards witch-spells, but to a very potent poison. If they press the matter further, there might be a chance that he even reveals a great plot twist: the girl is not really dead, but in a deep coma, as it seems magic was imbued in the poison. And, schooled in the ways of magic as he is he knows that all spells can be dispelled, all curses lifted.

Another find they might do at *Whitebay* are troll tracks on the scene, easy to follow to *Troll Cave*. If they pursue them, they will enter *Coille a Deas* (Southwood), where they may also find *Brigand Camp* and by the help of the brigands, *Secret Barn Entrance*.

If they successfully find *Troll Cave* they may fight or persuade the trolls to reveal what they found at the crime scene: a black and delicately crafted vial. If they bring it to the apothecary in *Flowerdale*, she will be able to say that there are traces of a magic-imbued poison in it.

Secret Barn Entrance can be found with the help of Ida Hayleah and the brigands, and it leads to the *Hidden Torture Cellar* of the Cairlin Estate. Here, they will very clearly understand that there is more to the Cairlins than anyone in Flowerdale might know, or want to for that part.

The chapter ends in a report in secrecy to Tearlach who reacts differently depending on the thoroughness of the player's investigation.

Experience Points are awarded at the end of Act I. The characters get following amounts of XP:
- 10 XP per Game Night (4-6 hrs game time).
- 10 XP for finding the poison vial and revealing its contents.
- 20 XP for exploring *Mordoc's "Fishing" Shack,* finding out that the girl is not murdered by a witch. +40 XP if the players manage to persuade the necromancer into revealing that Miranda is in fact not dead.
- 10 XP for succeeding in allying themselves with the brigands who show them the *Secret Barn Entrance*.

Act II: Revealing the Truth

The proceedings of the first trial can be read at page 26. If enough evidence has been gathered before the arrival of Lord Captain Nathair Falconer, it will result in his growing interest, and at the first trial, he will not consent to the accusations aimed at Ellen the Housemaid, but instead demand the matter be looked further into. His suspicions are shared by the players, Tearlach Cairlin, Thomir Belltower and two of the three First Leaders. And so, Nathair Falconer demands access to the *Cairlin Estate* for himself and the player characters, as they have already proven themselves to be valuable detectives. He will not listen to accusations of torture chambers as they are simply too outrageous to believe, and refuses to investigate the matter in respect to the landlords. However, First Leader Ida Hayleah may be persuaded.

Now things start to get complicated, as the actions of the player characters causes reactions in both evil characters and good, and thus there will be no single way storyline from here on. The important part is that the Game Master must try their utmost to outplay and outsmart the players as the evil characters: Eileen, Brodan and Liara. How the whole story will end is entirely dependant on the acts by the players and the managing of NPC:s by the Game Master. However, there are some main endings that may help the Game Master to better structure this act.

Righteous Ending

In this ending, the player characters manage to find a priest of Nidesfarn at *Fionn Gaithlean* who dispels Miranda, returning her to life. She is kept safe and hidden from view until the last trials are done, for her protection. During the trials, Baron and Baroness Cairlin are found guilty of vampirism and the subsequent torture and murder of innocent people, plotting against free will marriage and false accusations. They will be transferred to Caislean Uisce for detention and execution by fire mage. Liara will be sent to the front lines in the west to fight against the blackbloods, her crime only being plotting against free will marriage. The act will end happily with a marriage between the new Lord and Lady of Cairlin Estate. They will release Ellen from servitude leading to her becoming a successful artillery captain and later a skilled siege engineer stationed at the duke's side at Brianil, - a bastion in the capital city of Usentil.

Liara could not return to Flowerdale. In fact, she could not return to anywhere since she had been cursed with eternal undeath as a vampire. But her will to repent her former sins and her new-found purpose in life – the protection of her own people by sword – prevailed. She became one of the few good vampires, cursed to forever walk alone and to feed on the blood of the living. She chose to fight the daily inner battles against the creeping darkness which would one day subdue her and turn her to the evil side of the threshold. She killed many orcs and saved many hunter groups finding themselves in dire straits west of the Harg mountains and became widely known but never identified. Before she turned sinister she disintegrated her body in a horrendous blacksand detonation at one of the greater orc encampments, releasing her soul from the undead body by fire, as was the only salvation. Henceforth, her spirit would roam the slopes of the dales in eternal unrest, warning fighters of the three realms of ambushes and blackblood movements through her chilling nightly howls, and so she became known as *Scread Chraite* – Banshee Wail. After several centuries she was at last released from her eternal unrest by one of goddess Nikea's water spirits, who forgave her of her sins and helped her spirit over into the long-awaited afterlife.

Stories would turn Miranda Cairlin into legend, passing from one generation to the next; a tale of a simple maid falling in love with a baron, jealously put to a supposed death by her sister, only to rise again by the power of love and the skill of a few adventurers who believed in goodness. And so, she became known as the *"Maid of Flowerdale"*, a proud part of the Cairlin lineage, propelling them away from their dark past into a loving, wonderful future. Together with Tearlach, they continued to keep Flowerdale as it was, a beautiful town surrounded by lush woods abundant with life. Tearlach gracefully served in the wars against the blackbloods and returned whole, Miranda had many children and continued to live her life as she had always done – walking through the woods, collecting berries, greeting people in the streets of Flowerdale, visiting her father often. The only exception being of course her slightly more glorious residence as well as the occasional meetings and noble courts she needed to attend! She forgave her sister Liara, who needed a long time to come to terms with herself, but ultimately, got over it and found new purpose to the west. Miranda would get the central place and the largest portrait painting in the Cairlin Estate - a new beginning for the family; a symbol for what it had become. An eternal message that love – love conquers all.

Sorrowful Ending

The Baroness and Baron are found guilty of vampirism, torture, murder, plotting against free will marriage and lying under court oath. They are summarily to be executed at Caislean Uisce by fire mage. Liara is sentenced to death by burning with immediate effect and Ellen is freed and compensated for having been unjustly detained. The manorial court has proven (almost) righteous, and it would not have been without the help of the skilled adventurers. They receive the rewards by a gloomy, depressed Tearlach, now allowing himself to mourn the passing of his beloved. Miranda is buried (alive but in a coma) and will never awake due to no antidote being given her, and dies in her sleep in her coffin, her soul woeful and angry, doomed to haunt the Flowerdale graveyard for all eternity. She would become known as the *"Maid of Flowerdale"*, a title whispered in low voices during chill nights to scare children and adults alike.

Grey Ending

Miranda is brought back to life at *Fionn Gaithlean* and testifies in the second trial as eye-witness. Liara is found guilty of Plotting against free will marriage, Theft, Infringement on manorial grounds, Lying at Court, Framing of a Lady of the House, Framing of a Servant, and Assault. Since the players did not find the *Hidden Torture Cellar*, Liara's accusations towards Eileen's involvement in the plot fall mute due to the Baroness' significantly higher station. Ellen is freed of accusations and compensated for having been unjustly detained, and Liara is sentenced to prolonged service in the Perpetual War. Tearlach and Miranda get to marry each other, but Eileen and Brodan continues to roam free, forever darkening the region with their vampiric presence. In due time, once Miranda conceived, they would turn their son and her into vampires as well, extending the power of the Night Court of Wolfstone, increasing its influence in the upper echelons of alerian society. The Maid of Flowerdale never became folklore and was quickly sucked into the swift currents of oblivion, as each new morning turned slightly greyer after each passing night.

Black Ending

Not having found enough evidence, or the Baroness simply being too clever in her sly accusations at court, poor Ellen the Housemaid is found guilty as was believed all along. Liara is ordered down to the prison to watch Ellen so that she can not escape, but what Eileen truly had in mind was something completely different. She managed to make a pact with Mordoc the Necromancer, who showed up and bound Liara with a masterful Bind Soul battle of wills. He defeats the already weakened Liara, and she becomes his undying thrall. Ellen is brought to the courtyard and summarily executed by Lord Captain Nathair himself as custom demanded. Her heart was torn out while still alive so that her soul did not have time to escape into the area and it was thrown into a vat of burning embers, thought to scare the witch's soul far into the deeper reaches of the Shadow world. The players are dishonourably discharged by an enraged Tearlach cursing at the fate neither Miranda nor he deserved, threating them to be killed on sight if they dared show themselves in Faerann Eadar ever again. Miranda is buried, but the grave reopened, the Baroness fulfilling her end of the bargain she made with Liara. But Miranda would never live the life that was promised; she became a slave girl to a jarl at a backwater hamlet somewhere close to the Wastelands and would give birth, against her will, to three bastards whom in turn was doomed into serfdom in the harsh class-society of the Vorgar. Poor Ellen's soul did not run away from the region since she was innocently executed. Rather the opposite; her unrestful spirit roamed free in the estate grounds, tormenting visitors and residents alike, and became known as the *"Maid of Flowerdale"*, the vengeful ghost of a girl unjustly executed for crimes she never committed, haunting people's dreams in the dead of the night.

Experience Points are awarded at the end of Act II. The characters get following amounts of XP:
- 10 XP per Game Night (4-6 hrs game time).
- 100 XP for the *Righteous Ending*.
- 75 XP for the *Sorrowful Ending*.
- 70 XP for the *Grey Ending*.
- 10 XP for the *Black Ending*.

Main Characters

Non-combatant: Never performs any offensive or defensive damaging actions and actively avoids attackers.
Combatant, Defensive: Performs defensive damaging actions.
Combatant, Offensive: Performs offensive and defensive damaging actions and actively seeks out other combatants.

Miranda Belltower
Age: 20
Non-Combatant
Human, Alerian
Allegiance: Crown of Noralac
Relations: Liara Belltower (sister), Thomir Belltower (father), Tearlach Cairlin (betrothed)
Locations: Mordoc's "Fishing" Shack, Fionn Gaithlean, Cairlin Estate

Personality
Much has already been said about Miranda. She is a sweet girl with a loving and naïve heart, and she is the story's main focal point. She is very beautiful, with a long black hair, golden skin and slender body. She is social and creative but at the same time thoughtful and caring. She wishes the best for everyone and is polite towards strangers. Miranda lacks leadership and fast decision-making capabilities and does tend to become easily stressed in scary situations. She has a long patience but feels out of place in the upper echelons of alerian society.

Progress summary
Miranda is rendered unconscious and put into a magic-induced coma by her sister at the shores of Whitebay, mere hours away from Flowerdale, before the adventure starts. She may be saved by being transferred to a small chapel of the Sigan faith and dispelled by the priest there, Genadios Agate. She is not interactable until she is dispelled. *Miranda may not be rid of the spell by a simple Dispel cast by a mage, since a curse-lock is in place before the powerful magic. Only a divine plea followed by a skilled Dispel will reawaken Miranda.*

Lifting her curse, keeping her safe
If dispelled, Miranda is nauseous and confused, and need some time to rest. After that, the memories of what happened to her at Whitebay are sporadic at best. She remembers her sister forcing down the contents of the poison vial and has a faint memory of being held by her in her arms. She will say this at court in honesty, but she will also try to downplay the severity of Liara's crime. She still loves her, and when she realizes that Liara too loves Tearlach, her sympathy for her is only increased. Even though she would never have done the same, she understands that love can make anyone rash and desperate.

She will have an almost frantic urge to go to Tearlach as soon as she feels well enough (takes two days) to walk, but it is extremely important that her whereabouts remain unknown, because the Baroness is looking for her body as well. Should Eileen discover where she is, and furthermore that she is alive even, she will send Brodan to personally detain her and force her out of the realm, as planned.

Reuniting with Tearlach, attending the final trial
Miranda will stay at the chapel until the day of the final trial. After she reunites shortly with Tearlach in private, the trial commences. There, she is more a bystander than an active part of it. She is addressed but can not answer many questions. If her sister is sentenced to death for being a vampire however, Miranda cries out against the charge, pleading to the court to spare her sister. Ultimately though, she will not be heard, for justice is justice in Broadland and Liara must pay the price for having turned to the dark side no matter if it was forced upon her or not.

Reuniting with Tearlach is the happiest day of her life, succeeded by her new happiest day of her life: the wedding day. She will forever be grateful to the players for what they did for her and Tearlach. A feeling of undying love engulfs the players, permanently adding +1 to their Resolve.

Liara Belltower

Age: 24
Non-Combatant
Vampire (human), Alerian
Allegiance: Crown of Noralac
Relations: Miranda Belltower (sister), Thomir Belltower (father), Tearlach Cairlin (love-interest), Eileen Cairlin (partner-in-crime)
Locations: Flowerdale, Cairlin Estate

Personality

Liara had to shoulder a lot of responsibility in her youth as she was the older sister in the house of a widowed father. She was often accused of causing trouble made by Miranda and she found her younger sister teasing and testing, but it was never anything more than ordinary sibling rivalry. She took on her role stoically and did in a way feel at home as the mother figure Miranda needed. She came to realize though, as they grew up, that Miranda was to be the beautiful, extrovert and nice one, while she, even though averaging above many others on the beauty scale, was considered the somber, strict and boring one of the two. She secretly disliked that about Miranda as she stole the attention of men and women alike away from her, making her feel unwanted. As a result, she became insecure. Even though there were many occasions she hated her sister, in the end, she felt pure love towards her. She never hit her or tried ruining her sister's relations until the fateful day they both fell in love with Tearlach. Something changed in Liara, the weight of her love for the young lord seemingly forcing the love she held for Miranda away from the main reaches of her heart. Acting out of desperation, her feelings confused and blurry, she agreed on Eileen's plan to poison her sister just to detain her long enough for Tearlach to overcome his grief, and maybe start to develop feelings to the one who was of the same blood and similar looks as she.

Her world broke when she forced the poison down her sister's throat. Not only does she bear the burden of a murderess, she is also betrayed and at the same time bound to Eileen Cairlin. She was deceived but is in a helpless position: she cannot confess her crime and unravel the Baroness' part in the scheme, because she would be put to death by alerian law, but at the same time, she despises her. But more than anything she despises herself and a noticeable depression shadows her face. She is uncooperative and avoiding in conversation, and simply choose to not reply on too pressing and uncomfortable queries.

It was critical that Eileen made her a vampire so she was able to loosen the worst feelings of guilt as her soul became supressed under a veil of darkness, because now at least she can control her guilt.

Progression summary

Liara can be found in Flowerdale village, mostly at her father's house. She is approachable but passively hostile towards the players. She will not offer much in the way of help and keep to her and Eileen's story as far as possible. It is however quite easy to see that there is more to Liara than meets the eye. Something dark and looming. She looks troubled. After the first trial, upon the arrival of Lord Captain Nathair and the first manorial court, she will retreat to the estate grounds at the Baroness' behest and becomes harder to have access to. She spends most of her time hiding in a guest room, but sometimes she sits in the garden. The players might have gained full access to the estate due to Lord Captain Falconer demanding it, if they performed well during the first manorial court. Otherwise, they will have to sneak in and use stealth to find Liara, and if they do, she will try her best to alert the lord's men to arrest the trespassers.

At the second (last) manorial court, if Liara is found guilty for plotting against free will marriage, she is sent off to the frontlines in the Harg mountains where the Alerians fight the never-ending war against the blackbloods. She will accept this fate, as her guilt for what she'd done to her sister is still strong.

If she is found guilty of vampirism, she will confess the meeting between her and Eileen, and how she was shackled and forced into undeath, unable to resist. This does not lessen the court's resolve, even though pity may be seen on some member's faces. She is sentenced to death by Iron Ring, and as the sentence fall, she slumps down crying, regretting everything she'd done as a part of this horrid tale. Not even the corrupting undead magic in her heart could supress these feelings.

First Questioning of Liara

If the players confront Liara early in the game she will tell the made-up story of the supposed witch attack, promising them she saw at least someone looking very familiar to Ellen, also adding that clear evidence points towards Ellen in the tuft of blonde hair and the copper necklace. She will try her utmost to keep the secret, and no telepathic spells or other chants work on her. She will not budge to charm attempts or bribes, she will remain as silent as the grave if pressed too hard.

Second Questioning of Liara

By this time, the players should have made progress, finding new evidence that clearly competes with her story. She is now inclined to reply at least in part to the player's discoveries, and tries her utmost to play it defensively, all the while sticking to her story. She has answers to all discoveries:

The Poison Vial

Since it was not discovered at the beach, it is far from certain the trolls nicked it, making it end up in their cave. As far as she knows it may have been stolen from someone's larder. Regardless, she reassures that as far as she remembered, there was no vial involved in the witch attack. If the players managed to get a troll to confess that it did indeed find the vial at the beach, Liara simply stares in disbelief - who in their right mind would take anything a troll said as truth?

Necromancer Autopsy

She stares blankly upon hearing about the supposed examination of her sister at the hands of a necromancer. Everyone knows necromancers are madmen and conducts experiments on dead and live alike. Liara demands to know why the players did not try to apprehend the obvious enemy of the people and turns the situation to her favour, also scolding them for not retrieving Miranda's body.

Torture Cellar

Her eyes go wide but she quickly regains her composure. She asks them how they dare come up with such horrid fantasies, how they dare accuse the Lord and Lady of the house with such terrible lies.

Presented to Miranda

If she is secretly persuaded to go and see her supposedly alive sister and realize the truth of her being alive, she will break. She will ask her sister for forgiveness and stay true to her word to testify at court against Baroness Cairlin and explain their dark scheme. She will not confess being a vampire, as it would surely cost her life.

Roughed up

The players will not gain anything by being bad to her, hitting her, even torturing her. That will only strengthen her resolve and create a disdain in her towards the players.

Lord Tearlach Cairlin

Age: 27
Combatant, Offensive
Human, Alerian
Allegiance: Crown of Noralac
Relations: Miranda Belltower (betrothed), Baron Brodan Cairlin (father), Baroness Eileen Cairlin (mother)
Locations: Flexible, but in larger part, he is found at the Cairlin Estate

STR: 14	END: 16	DEX: 12	SWI: 12	INT: 15
WIS: 10	RES: 18	CHA: 17	AWA: 12	

Life Points: 100 Recovery: 20 LP/day   Damage mod. +1   Movement: 4 meters/AP   AP: 5/BR

Fear Mod. +6   Reaction: +1   Resilience: 7

Full Heavy Armour: 5 DV. Adorned with the Cairlin crest: A round red serpent on a dark green background. Wields a one-handed longsword named *Claidhean Gleannach (Sword of the Dales)*, which does 2d6+3 damage.

Skills	**Skill level**
Arms: Bows, One-handed Swords, Two-handed Swords	14
Shields: Medium Shields	12
Armours: Heavy Armour	19
Artillery: Ballista, Trebuchet	9
Combat Tactics	8
Economy	10
Geography: Grimlake, Wayland	10
Heraldry: Alerians	16
History: Alerians, Orcs	13
Hunt	16
Laws and Rights: Broadland	15
Leadership	18
Riding: Horse	13
Society and Culture: Broadland	10
Trading	8

Personality

Tearlach is the typical extrovert commander "good prince" archetype. He is confident, good looking and of noble birth. He is inspiring and creative, a man of action and brilliance. The news of Miranda's death does not force him into complete despair, his willpower so strong it overcomes even the shock of total loss. He is enraged at the cruel fate of his beloved and will go through fire to get to the bottom of what happened at Whitebay. He cares little of Liara's testimony, he wants to know where Miranda's corpse went and exactly what happened. He creates an investigation of his own, his intelligence forcing him to think clear and realize he needs help. He hires the companions and they become his crime investigation partners. He expects them to report their findings to him first and will be furious should the players do otherwise. Forceful as he is when he wants his will, he also demands results from the investigation. Should the players fail in accumulating new leads, he will regard them with contempt similar to that of his mother.

Tearlach is a man of good judgement and strong determination. He is not one for using his power to elevate himself above others, but at the same time he does use it when the need arises, and thus he is still considered a noble in its exact meaning by the people of Flowerdale. Religion has never been central in his life, but he respects the spirits and gods, and does not particularly dislike the Sigan faith that has been growing in influence since the War of Fear. He has a fascination for magic and will be positively thrilled should one of the player characters be a mage.

Recruiting the companions

Tearlach will be upfront and frank with the players, stating his urgent need for investigators that are not from the region. He provides information about the murder: that he was to be Miranda's husband, that she went away to Whitebay with

her sister, but that only her sister Liara returned and that according to her they had been attacked by a witch. Problem was, Liara had already approached his mother, Baroness Eileen, with a tuft of hair and a copper necklace that she apparently managed to rip off of this witch in the fight. His mother had recognized the necklace and demanded the maid Ellen be brought forward for questioning. Upon closer inspection of the girl, a part of her golden hair was indeed missing, the golden tuft fitting perfectly, and when they presented the copper necklace to her, she confirmed it was hers. And so, it all pointed towards this maid, but Tearlach felt there was something amiss. The naivety of Ellen, how confused she appeared to be to the whole situation, told him that just maybe she should be given the benefit of a doubt. And there were many questions unanswered: where was Miranda's corpse? What injuries did it sustain? Where was Ellen's hideout in the woods? How many more had she killed? And was it really a coincidence that Miranda short before her marriage with him was the target of a random witch attack? Tearlach tells the players that he asked these same questions at the first court meeting, and since they could not all be answered he demanded the matter to be judged by higher authority and had thus sent a letter pigeon to the Lord Captain of Faerann Eadar: Lord Nathair Falconer requesting his presence at the manorial court at the Cairlin Estate. He hoped Miranda's close relationship to him would prove sufficient enough to grant Lord Falconer's appearance. Successfully suspending judgement of the girl until answer arrived, he immediately set off to Whitebay where he found lots of tracks and signs that there had been a tumult, but he did not find Miranda's body. Even though he desperately wanted to continue the search for her, he knew he had to get back to the estate before the letter pigeon returned. He had an urge to personally receive the answer, he did not want anyone else's hands on it. Shortly after his return to the estate, the pigeon returned with a letter signed by Lord Falconer. If the players ask if they could see it, Tearlach will show it to them. It reads:

Request for presence at the Cairlin Estate due to Witch Trial

Dear Lord Tearlach, son of Baron Cairlin
It is not common that I partake in trials of such a minor importance as that of Witches in the woodlands of Faerann Eadar. I have full confidence these matters are supremely handled by the lesser authorities, such as thyself and thine elders. However, I understand that thou were close to the girl now undone - that she was to be thine wife. As such, I shall make an exception, and gracefully accept thine invitation to the Manorial Court at thine Estate. I have a few matters that needs tending before I may take leave from my Duties at Caislean Uisce. I shall arrive in two days from now. I trust thou make the most of the time until my arrival.

Lord Captain Nathair Falconer, Count's Second of the Fair County of Faerann Eadar

Tearlach tells the players the letter was received yesterday evening, meaning they have approximately two days to find more clues as to Miranda's fate. Tearlach makes no secret that he has to stay at the estate to prevent rash decisions. The town is shaken by this loss and Thomir Belltower, Miranda's father, more than anyone. Tearlach needs eyes at Whitebay, eyes in the woods, and most importantly, brains that may roam freely in the region. As a reward for solving this mystery and finding the body of his betrothed, he offers the players 10 gold coins as well as a Raven Duty emblem – a medal given to those who has shown great resolve and helpfulness to one or more nobles of the realms. A mid-tier medal as far as medals go in the three realms. He will not give up his persuasion attempts until the players have accepted his quest.

Before the first trial

Tearlach expects to receive a full report on the finds the players make during the initial two days prior to Lord Captain Falconers arrival and the awaited first trial. He needs evidence that suggests Ellen might be innocent. During those two days, he tries to help the players as best he can. For example, he may lend them mules for carrying equipment and three horses (whom he owns personally). He can also provide them with one Longsword each (on loan) and if they ask, he will give them 200 arrows or bolts for free, paid for from his own coffer. He does not have authority enough to grant them entry to his parent's estate grounds and cannot lend any guards to accompany them since they have sworn fealty to Baron Brodan, his father, and not him. All in all he does not have more power than to stall the trials, make sure nothing happens to Ellen the Accused and providing the players with above equipment.

Reactions on evidence

Depending on the evidence the players are able to provide, Tearlach reacts differently. Needless to say, he endorses all evidence pointing towards the murderer being anyone else than Ellen whom he firmly believes is innocent. However, there are limits to what he believes. All in all, this is what he will be carrying with him to the first trial. *Only if the players have found no evidence other than Brigand's claims of a secret torture chamber will he concede defeat, allowing judgement to be passed onto Ellen. If the players managed to find the poison vial, Miranda's body at Mordoc's "Fishing" Shack or both, he will press the matter further in defence of Ellen, leading to Lord Captain Falconer declaring another trial in ten days, in order to fully investigate these leads.*

Poison Vial

He turns to Lord Captain Falconer with a grave look on his face clearly showing he believes there is more to this story than Liara claims. The troll tracks at the site cannot rule out the possibility that the trolls took the vial from the scene. (If the players managed to press information from the trolls in *Troll Cave*, they even tell them that they took the vial from the beach and that they saw no girl there. Tearlach mentions this as well as cause to postpone the execution of Ellen until matters are fully resolved.)

Brigand's claim of torture chambers

He is not at all amused of these claims and have no choice really other than to deny his house' involvement in such grisly affairs. Beyond closed doors that is. They have publicly detained witches in the past, it was part of their responsibility as a noble estate to the people of the region, and torture was sometimes included as a just punishment for those who had wronged enough victims to receive it. Additionally, he does not support any claims coming from outlaws, and dismisses their claims that the estate would house any secrets. (By this time Tearlach is innocently unaware of his parents being vampires and their secret dungeon beneath the estate cellar.) The only explanations he sees at that moment is that the brigands weave lies around their estate prison, and promptly withholds, as this trial obviously shows, that the Cairlins take great care to not pass judgement on innocent people. He has not heard of any "Secret entrances" to his estate.

Miranda's body being found

Regardless of how the players play this out, Tearlach naturally burst with emotions. He demands that he be shown the body of his beloved but can be persuaded to wait if the players swear that she is still alive and can be saved. He believes their story, the same that Mordoc the Necromancer provided for them: that the necromancer found the body of the girl a stone throw from his "fishing shack", and as he thought her dead wanted to experiment on her, maybe raise her corpse. Talking about this evokes strong feelings in Tearlach; at one moment he wants to strangle the old man with his bare hands just to calm down the next moment, realizing the necromancer may be an invaluable witness to the whole murder mystery.

Miranda's autopsy

In fact, Mordoc never performs an autopsy on Miranda. As he inspected the body it was revealed no external wounds was inflicted, and no internal bleedings could be seen as black marks on her body. He did however find signs of poisoning in her oesophagus, and interestingly, her body temperature was slightly above that of a corpse. Her lips were not black, her skin, golden as it was, not as deathly white as that of a dead woman. His conclusion was that she was alive and that she must have been forced to drink a highly potent sleeping poison. If the players managed to coax this information out of Mordoc, regardless if they choose to let her be monitored by the old man or transported in secrecy back to Flowerdale, Tearlach demands he be allowed to see her. If this happens before the first trial or after makes no difference for the fact that Tearlach realizes that Liara's tale is obviously a lie. And so, he also understands the need for subtlety and that Miranda's whereabouts must remain unknown to anyone at court as they do not yet know who is behind all this. An important evidence is laid bare before Tearlach, solidifying his position as Ellen's defender: Miranda was poisoned by a poison vial and is alive - she was not attacked and killed by a witch, regardless if this housemaid named Ellen in fact turns out to be a witch or not. His suspicions are directly aimed at Liara, the only eye-witness from the scene. Did she poison her sister? Why would she, and also, where did she get the enchanted poison vial? He suggests Miranda be transported to the only safe location he is aware of, namely *Fionn Gaithlean* – the Sigan chapel seven kilometres due northeast of Ashbow, the middlemost town in the county. They do not have time for this before the first trial and must undertake the trip after the trial.

Tearlach during the first trial

Tearlach will support the players and defend Ellen if the players have produced one of the two main evidences conflicting with Liara and Eileen's evidence. The players must have gained the *Poison Vial* from the *Troll Cave,* or the body investigation by Mordoc at *Mordoc's "Fishing" Shack* to convince Tearlach to continue the defence of Ellen. The

third evidence provided by the Brigands, that his House have hidden dungeons beneath their estate is frowned upon as he firmly, yet falsely, believes that it is merely rumours being spread by outlaws and defectors in the regions to besmirch their good name. If the only evidence is the Brigand's revealing of the *Secret Barn Entrance* to the players, he *will not support* any further defence of Ellen, forcing Lord Captain Falconer to sentence the innocent housemaid to death by "Witchsoul abolishment", a hideous execution method where the witch is tied firmly to a rack, wheel or other contraption, and the executioner then cuts out their still beating heart, promptly throwing it into a burning vat in front of the accused, that they may witness their own heart sizzling in their last moments in life.

Hopefully all goes well, leading to Tearlach demanding that the player characters be allowed full access to the estate and houses, private or official. He is granted this by Lord Captain Falconer with additional support by First Leaders Ida Hayleah and Bordrin Somersburn, with neutral support by Town Reeve Thomir Belltower.

Before the second trial

During this time Tearlach will undertake the trip to *Mordoc's "Fishing" Shack* and onwards. He has to choose between moving straight for the chapel through the thick underbrush of *Coille a Deas* or the easier country road – a wide detour (in distance at least) through the towns of *Fairwood Glen* and *Ashbow,* ending the journey at *Fionn Gaithlean* – a temple dedicated to the Sigan father of all Gods: Nidesfarn. He is overcome with a fear-mixed joy upon seeing his beloved Miranda again, but he worries greatly. Will the enaxian priests at the chapel really be able to cure his Miranda? Or is she cursed to forever sleep in a living death? He asks the player characters to join him as an escort, as he could not grant Miranda's safety all by himself. He urges them so promptly they really do not have any other choice than to follow.

During this part of the quest the companions may run into encounters not specifically tied to the main story. Tearlach wants to press on, but allows some respite to let the players explore as long as they do it fast.

If they succeed in transporting Miranda to the chapel (the journey will take approximately one day one way regardless of choice). The *Country Road* choice is twenty kilometres long, while the *Road through Coille a Deas* is only thirteen kilometres, but because of rough terrain, it will be slower going.

Once they reach *Fionn Gaithlean* they are met by the simple Nidesfarn priest Genadios Agate of the enaxian empire. He will dispel the prolonged poison with a blessed antidote said to have been bestowed upon the faithful by Nikea, Queen Goddess and Matron of the Seas. It worked, and a groggy Miranda opened her eyes to Tearlach's unfathomable joy. He is overcome with emotions but brings himself under control, understanding the priest's urge of letting her rest and recover. He commands the player characters back to his estate, urging them to delve deeper into this attempted murder or whatever it was. Now, Tearlach begins wondering about his parents, Liara and the whole business surrounding him and his marriage with Miranda. He himself decides to stay by the bed of his beloved, for he could not suffer her security by leaving her alone again.

Tearlach during the second trial

Because of the many possibilities which vary greatly upon the progression of the players, Tearlach reacts in far too many ways that it is meaningful to write them all down. To summarize Tearlach, he will defend Ellen if the following has been achieved:
1. There was enough evidence during the first trial to support a new trial.
2. He has been allowed to see Miranda.
3. The players have been successful in finding out that the content of the vial was actually a paralyzing poison.
4. The players have proof of the existence of hidden torture chambers beneath the estate.

Tearlach will, at a loss of words, support the accusations made against his parents for being vampires if the following has been achieved:
1. The players have proof of the existence of hidden torture chambers (and one or two living victims) beneath the estate.
2. Liara confesses her involvement, Eileen's plot and she turning her into a vampire against her will.

Tearlach will be forced to lay down his defence of poor Ellen if there is insufficient evidence of an assassination attempt from someone else than the witch Ellen, and has no other choice than to support the accusers. This will only happen if the players have been unable to establish that Miranda is alive.

If the players successfully manage to persuade the court that Liara did poison her sister, Eileen will turn on her, stating that with this new revelation, it is obviously she who is the murderess! During the following accusations from his mother, Tearlach has no other choice than to defend Ellen and accuse Liara for murdering her sister – his betrothed, leading to her execution by fire performed by Fordron the wizard, ordered there by Lord Captain Falconer once judgement is passed.

Tearlach during the end of the adventure

How Tearlach behaves towards the player characters is highly dependant on the outcome of the adventure itself. See pages 14-15 for information about the possible endings.

Baroness Eileen Cairlin

Age: 49
Combatant, Offensive
Vampire, First of the Cairlin Bloodline
Allegiance: Night Court of Wolfstone
Relations: Brodan Cairlin (husband), Tearlach Cairlin (son)
Locations: Cairlin Estate

| STR: 10 | END: 17 | DEX: 9 | SWI: 12 | INT: 18 |
| WIS: 16 | RES: 18 | CHA: 17 | AWA: 18 | |

Life Points: 94 (Vampire: when killed, the body begins normal Recovery until healed. Upon reaching maximum Life Points, the vampire rises again. Only way to kill a vampire is by banishing its soul, or binding it to an item, place or will.)

| Recovery: 20 LP/day | Spell Points: 136 | SP Recovery: 34 | Movement: 4 meters/AP |
| AP: 5/BR | Fear Mod. +6 | Reaction: +4 | Resilience: 7 |

Skills	Skill level
Alchemy	14
Astronomy	8
Botany	14
Charm	16
Criminal Underworld	20
Diplomacy	6
Economy	15
Extracts	13
Heraldry: Alerians	17
Laws and Rights: Broadland	18
Riding	10
Society and Culture: Alerians	17
Sorcery	16
Trading	10
Trickery	16

Ability: *Blood Baroness*
Eileen Cairlin heals for 50% of all damage done by her.

Sorcery Spells	Spell level	Page (*Vindeon – An Adventure Role-playing Game*)
Nerve Surge	3	234
Sunder	3	234
Heartburst	2	234
Enslave	4	235
Strangulate	2	235
Move Object	2	238
Move Self	3	238
Transcend Object	2	239
Transcend Self	1	239
Veil of Darkness	4	242

Trickery Spells	Spell level	Page
Dampen Light	4	223
Mute	1	231

Personality

Eileen Cairlin is the main antagonist in this adventure. She is responsible for turning Liara against her sister and carrying out the successful poisoning attempt on Miranda, she is responsible for the murders of innocent victims, both those that she and her husband catch in the night in the countryside for feeding and those they frame and accuse of witchcraft when the populace starts to react to the many disappearances with fear and suspicion. The framing of Ellen the housemaid was carried out by her alone; she snuck into the maid's chamber, stole her necklace and cut off the golden lock she was later to give Liara. And she has power which she uses to the utmost extent and she does so excellently. In spite of all her cunning and schemes, it seems she has made a fateful error though; she has underestimated her son's willpower and determination. To her irritation, Tearlach seems to have taken it upon himself to go to the bottom of this murder mystery, his love for Miranda much deeper than Eileen ever thought possible. Thus, she is at a slight disadvantage: though confident that she will succeed in ridding the world of Miranda, or at least neutralize her so she will not marry her son, she still needs to prevent the private investigators (player characters) to finding out the truth. She can not do this openly, but on the other hand, it is behind closed doors she excels.

The Baroness is a typical evil stepmother character, with the important addition that she is a vampire. Play her passively aggressive, mean and superior to the players, and forthcoming and smirking towards higher nobles or honoured guests (such as the members of the manorial court). She is highly intelligent, so it is important the GM plays her smart and designing. She rarely makes mistakes, and when she does, she will do her best to minimize their impact on her schemes. Eileen looks down on people. You can see it in her eyes; they are cold and uncaring, a darkness poorly hidden in the midst of extravagant, rich clothing and sweet perfumes. She likes to hold things in her right hand all the time, and her favourite item is her obsidian-infused golden goblet, in which she often pours wine, frequently mixed with a few drops of blood to keep her "fresh".

Eileen only really cares for two things: herself and power. Therefore, she needs her bloodline strong and in high esteem throughout the realms. For now, her allegiance is to the Night Court of Wolfstone – a gathering of greater vampires of high standing within the Realm of Noralac, ruled by Count Iorval Wolfstone, the same man who had given her the Kiss of Death when she visited him whilst investigating the strange disappearance of her brother. How ironic it is that her own son now has embarked on a similar investigation! Being turned into a vampire did not change Eileen much – she was an arrogant, mean woman already before she was turned into a vampire. However, what she gained was that which she sought the most: immortality. Powerful spells quickly came to her mind as the void energies of Illsvinn swirled around her. Indeed, her "unfortunate" run-in with the good count had proven more than advantageous. The only problem was that she would become unable to conceive another child, and so the importance of Tearlach producing capable heirs became more important to Eileen. She would not suffer her son marrying anyone even remotely close to being unimportant, and she decided that he was to marry no lesser lady than a Baroness or Knightly Dame. Imagine her disbelief when her son announced he would marry Miranda, youngest daughter of the insignificant reeve of Flowerdale, a town she in the clearest of definitions owned!

Pre-Adventure: Acquiring the poison

Through her contacts in the criminal underworld of Usentil, Capital of Noralac, Eileen managed to get a hold of an extremely potent paralyzing poison imbued with a spell trap set to trigger once the liquid was emptied, causing the victim's body to collapse, throwing it into a deep coma very closely resembling death. Eileen, when handing the vial over to Liara, called it a "sleeping potion", to minimize the chance of Liara getting second thoughts. The poison was, as someone might inquire, not bought from the shop of Mrs. Thornrose Venoma, Flowerdale's local apothecary, and so Thornrose was unaware of the poison. This means that there are no witnesses available to the transaction between Eileen and the seller whom the players can get a hold of in the region.

Before the first trial

During the time the players investigate possible leads leading them to one or more of the three areas *Troll Cave*, *Mordoc's "fishing" shack* and *Brigand Camp*, Eileen remains passive. She monitors the situation, confident that whatever comes out of it, she will emerge victorious. Her son's request for the esteemed Lord Captain of Faerann Eadar is a setback, but a minor one, and she knows that she will be able to defend Liara's innocence easily, especially in the face of such overwhelming evidence towards Ellen the housemaid. As a matter of fact, Eileen is in a bit of bad luck, both with the trolls and the necromancer living in the "fishing" shack. It annoyed her to some extent that Liara managed to leave the empty vial behind, but she could not foresee that trolls would have already searched the scene, found it, and taken it back to their cave before her outriders arrived to retrieve it. If the players managed to talk to the trolls, they revealed

that they found the vial on the beach, which would become problematic to explain during the first trial. Worse still, if the players managed to find the very body of Miranda in the hands of Mordoc the Necromancer, revealing she was not even dead, the physical examination pointing towards poisoning, not a powerful witch-spell, she would have even greater challenges in the coming trial. But Eileen was as cunning as she was wicked and would prove difficult to overcome.

Eileen during the first trial

When the court is seated, Eileen has a vast majority supporting Liara, her story and the evidence already laid bare incriminating Ellen being the malicious witch that had tried to take the lives of two local, innocent girls. Town-reeve Thomir supports his oldest daughter, grief burning in his eyes at the loss of his youngest daughter. Eileen's husband Baron Brodan supports the claims, for he is already involved and invested in the plot. Not that he is overly interested, leaving politics mostly to his wife, but he supports her nonetheless. First Leader John Wood was known for his witch-hate, having lost his only child to an old crone in the bogs east of Harg. He was the only first leader Eileen was able to place in the court. The other two – Ida Hayleah and Bordrin Somersburn, were too influential to replace with other puppets of hers. And so, they were neutral in the matter, as was Lord Captain Falconer. Against her she merely had her son and Ellen, who was confused and scared and denied that she knew anything about the witch attack on the sisters. The setting looked promising, but she could not foresee the detective skills of the player characters!

Proceedings of the first trial

The first trial is opened by Lord Captain Falconer bidding the accuser to step forward and proclaim the charges. Liara does so. She tells her version of what happened – that Ellen attacked her and her sister with a sinister spell that hit Miranda who dropped dead before her, sacrificing herself to protect her sister. Liara went into a fury like a cornered animal, managed to score a few hits and scratches and she managed to rip off the witch's necklace and a tuft of hair. The witch ran away, and when Liara came to her senses, she tried to wake Miranda – to no avail. She could not carry her all the way back to Flowerdale, and so, she ran as fast as she could to the estate, where she met Eileen whom she told what had just happened at Whitebay. When Liara presented the hair and necklace, Eileen recognized it, and later that evening, she had her guards arrest the maid and throw her into the prison.

To this, the Lord Captain bids Ellen to step forward. "Does the defender find these accusations accurate?" he inquires. Ellen shakes her head but does not dare to look upon such a noble man.

"No, most honoured Lord Captain" she dared to say. "I was not there."

"But this copper necklace – it belongs to you, does it not?" Falconer replied. The girl nodded.

"And this tuft of hair, would you say it could fit into the ripped-off patch on your head?" he continued.

Ellen began sweating, her heart rushing fast. "It is my hair. Although, I do not know how it ended up in this woman's hands." She was quick to add the last part.

"Thank you" the Lord Captain said, and the court turned inwards, discussing the matter for themselves. After a few moments, the Lord Captain turned towards Tearlach.

"Lord Tearlach Cairlin has decided to act as the girl's defendant. What can you say to suggest the girl's innocence?" Tearlach rises and presents the player characters to the court, stating that they are his investigators and have found new evidence which suggests there is another truth to the Whitebay incident. He lets them speak. Eileen or Liara will be able to refute many of their claims. This is Eileen's replies:

The trolls looted the poison vial

"There is nothing that suggests these strangers are telling us the truth. I do not doubt trolls may have been around the place of murder, attracted as they are to the scent of the dead, but no one can ever know truly if the trolls found the vial there. They might have found it in the woods or at the side of a road – no one knows. Even if they found it at the beach, what binds it to the attack? Many items are washed up on our fair beaches – I would imagine a vial might very well do the same.

The trolls told them where they found it

Eileen stares disdainfully at the player characters. "Only lunatics and creatures even more stupid than trolls would believe what trolls say" she replies with finality and wisdom. She skilfully remains quiet thereafter, letting the logic sink it to the others at court, who nods, some even smiling for such a silly evidence. Lord Captain Falconer however, does not.

The content of the vial is verified to have been a potent paralyzing poison

"There are many empty vials filled with all kinds of contents throughout the realms. What this has to do with this trial, I cannot fathom."

Necromancer Autopsy

For the first time, Eileen seems to be caught off guard, but she quickly recovers. Curse her estate guards for being unable to find this necromancer's hideout! She regains her composure and stares coldly at the player characters. "Well done. You have succeeded in finding our beloved Miranda where my own house guards failed. Now then, where is she?"

If the players tell her that they wish for Miranda's location to remain unknown because for the girl's own safety, Eileen scoffs in disapproval. "You would dare suggest the walls and swords of this house insufficient for Miranda's safety? She, who were to be wed with my own son?" The mood in the court becomes slightly colder, but Tearlach steps in:

"It is by my command Miranda's location remains unknown to all but me and my investigators. Clearly, there is something amiss, and even though the confines of our house are indeed well guarded, I feel more certain of her safety when she remains at an unknown location to those who seek to do her harm. We do not yet know what exactly happened, but I swear before the court that we shall find out soon enough."

This troubles Eileen significantly. She must find Miranda at all costs, kill her herself if need be, so that she could never give witness to the actual happenings, let alone manage to marry her son. By this time, she doubts that this trial will succeed in sentencing Ellen to death – too many questions remain.

Torture cellar

Sighs of disbelief is breathed by many of the assembled court members. This is outrageous and a great insult to the noble Cairlins. Even Tearlach reacts as if stung, and it seems as if he is beginning to wonder which side the player characters are on. Brodan steps in, letting Eileen lay back and enjoy the scolding (p. 33). After a while, Lord Captain Falconer bids the court to confer with him in private once more.

First Trial Outcomes

This is a crucial moment in the adventure. If the players have managed to accumulate enough evidence, the trial will be postponed, leading to the next act. Below are listed different combinations of evidence discovered by the players, and what consequences they will have upon the main storyline.

Poison Vial only

The evidence against Ellen are far superior than some empty poison vial retrieved from a troll's lair in the woods. And an eye-witness attest that it was Ellen who assaulted them and killed her sister. Ellen is sentenced to be subjected to *Witchsoul Abolishment* – a horrid method of executing witches – with the full support of the court, even Tearlach.

Torture Cellar only

Same as "Poison Vial only".

Necromancer Autopsy only

If the players assure the court that Miranda is still alive, Lord Captain Falconer decides, in opposition to Eileen, Brodan and John Wood, that the judgement be postponed until they have found out the truth of Miranda's fate. Should she be alive, she is an important eye witness. A second trial is scheduled to commence in ten days. If the players have only found Miranda and does not know she is alive but was told by Mordoc that Miranda appeared to have been poisoned, Lord Captain Falconer, with the general support of the court, declares the body be brought to the estate to undergo a new autopsy by a trusted alchemist; Apothecary Thornrose Venoma. The next trial is scheduled to commence in ten days.

Poison Vial and Necromancer Autopsy

Lord Captain Falconer is amused, his keen intellect not having to do much working to realize that this murder case may have potential to be more interesting than it first seemed. Two competing stories are now at display. On one side, there is Liara as eye witness and the belongings she alone acquired during the fight. On the other, there is a supposed poison vial from the scene and the very body of Miranda (thought dead or otherwise), and an examination by someone not present suggesting she was in fact poisoned, not killed by witch spells. Here, Eileen and Liara must bite their lips and give their support to Lord Captain Falconer, Thomir and Tearlach. Another trial is scheduled for ten days, and by then, Miranda's body should have been brought before the court or Apothecary Thornrose.

Poison Vial and Torture Cellar

A somewhat outraged court deems the evidence lacking to support Ellen's innocence. She is sentenced to death by Witchsoul Abolishment.

Eileen before the second trial

The adventure going to a second trial means that Miranda's body has been found, and therefore becomes Eileen's highest priority target. She sends outriders in the night to search Whitebay and nearby woods. She sends them to patrol the few villages on the roads; *Ashbow, Somersburn, Aine, Fairwood Glen* and, naturally, *Flowerdale*. The chances are high the player characters will encounter some of them during their journeys. On the second day after the first trial, they will find *Mordoc's "fishing" shack*. If the players have not moved Miranda away from there, they will find her and bring her back to the estate in secrecy. Eileen will discretely bury her under the stone floor in the secret dungeons beneath the estate, successfully eliminating the chance anyone will ever find out the truth of Tearlach and his investigator's claims that she was poisoned rather than killed.

The evil baroness cannot do much more than that and starts brooding. She comes up with a back-up plan, seeing as the tides are definitely turning against her. If the *Secret Barn Entrance* was compromised, she orders her soldiers to raze the several hundred meters long tunnel leading to the dungeons and fill the hole in the barn with tightly packed dirt indistinguishable from the ordinary floor. If Falconer or someone else would inspect the barn, they would not be able to detect a secret entrance anymore. She prepares to turn on Liara, should Tearlach's investigators actually return to the estate with Miranda.

Eileen during the second trial
Given that a second trial even was decided means that Eileen's first scheme failed. Also, it means that her attempts at foiling the player character's and Tearlach's endeavours during Act II in varying degrees has also failed. She attends the second trial at a disadvantage but has one ace up her sleeve.

No new evidence
If the players managed to get so far as being granted a second trial but failed in procuring any new evidence, Eileen has no other choice (nor will) than to find her housemaid Ellen guilty as charged. Pretending to be hurt, she looks at Ellen.

"Even though you have done us much harm, I cannot help but find it sad that such a young maid now must be punished so harshly. It is my duty by law to attend the execution, but I will find little joy in it, and spirits help me, that my will is strong enough to withhold tears from my cheeks." (Leads to *Black Ending*) p. 15.

Miranda's testimony only
If Miranda is brought before the court alive, she will testify against her sister, by simply telling the truth – she and her sister was alone on the beach and they were not attacked by a witch. Liara forced something down her throat and after that she passed out, not waking until being dispelled by the Sigan priest Genadios Agate.

To this, Eileen turns on her subject Liara. "Many years have I lived, but never until this day have I been more duped than by this cunning, evil woman!" she exclaims, pointing at Liara accusingly. "In good faith I believed her lies, her evidence – the necklace and hair of Ellen, one of my own housemaids, and it all seemed undisputable and true. But I have had growing suspicions as well, and this servant of darkness will no longer have my support! Yes, dear Lords and Ladies, I will go as far as to say I have figured her out completely!" (GM: Eileen casts a successful Mute spell on Liara) "She is guilty of framing an innocent girl and plotting against free will marriage by paralyzing her own sister! I do not know how she managed to sneak into the estate grounds and steal the lock of hair and Ellen's copper necklace. We shall see to it that the guards that were on duty that night are replaced immediately – the security of our servants are most important to us!" Eileen finishes, sits back relaxingly in her chair and allows herself a sip of her (GM: blood infused) wine. (GM: She releases Liara from her Mute spell.)

"Indeed, it seems the fog is lifting, allowing us all to see things clearer" Falconer proclaims. "The court shall deliberate. We will announce the next session shortly."

After a short brake allowing the judges time of their own, the court is reassembled. Falconer speaks:

"Substantive arguments and evidence points towards Liara being guilty of the following crimes: Plotting against free will marriage, Theft, Infringement on manorial grounds, Lying at Court and Assault. The court's reconstruction of Liara's acts will hereby be brought forth: It is the court's strong belief that Liara procured the vial of paralyzing poison illegally for own gains. She then managed to infiltrate the Cairlin Estate and procure the tuft of hair and the copper necklace from an unsuspecting, sleeping housemaid, which happened to be Ellen, in order to falsely frame her of being a witch, thereby freeing herself from suspicions. For reasons she will soon confess, Liara then lured Miranda away from Flowerdale to the secluded shores of Whitebay. There she assaulted her, forcing the contents of the vial down her throat, rendering her unconscious which Miranda has attested. Liara must have panicked or she might simply have been an amateur criminal, as she left Miranda's body on the shore and the empty vial alike. She went straight to the good baroness and acted roughed up and claimed she and her sister was attacked by a witch who supposedly killed her sister but failed to kill her as she defended herself. When presenting the tuft of hair and copper necklace to the good Baroness, she recognized them belonging to one of her servants; Ellen, and unknowingly, she wrongly had her detained, believing Liara and her apparent evidence. She would not fathom such a heinous act as poisoning one's own sister and thus she was fooled, no darkness upon her." The Lord Captain nodded apologizingly to Eileen, who appeared slightly shamed and worried.

"However," Falconer continued, "Liara did not foresee the persistence of Lord Tearlach Cairlin, who loved Miranda beyond any mortal realm. He hired investigators who performed outstandingly in finding evidence supporting the truth. They found Miranda and managed to dispel her paralysis by the divine aid at Fionn Gaithlean. They kept her safe from hostile actions. They found the poison vial and found out its contents with the aid of experts. And so, Liara made herself guilty of the above stated charges." Falconer turns towards Liara, who slumped in her chair. "Does the defendant find these claims true?"

Liara assembled courage, but the great burden of guilt weighed heavily upon her shoulders.

"I confess to all charges…" she said to a satisfied court, save her father Thomir who seemed significantly older and greyer. "…except theft and infringement on manorial grounds." Again, curious heads were raised towards each other. Eileen held her breath, a deathly, threatening gaze locking onto Liara. But Liara held firm.

"It was Baroness Cairlin's idea to replace Miranda as Tearlach's betrothed, and I can only imagine the reason being nothing more than Miranda not being of noble birth. I loved Tearlach more than anything, and by the time I agreed on poisoning my sister and received the vial from Baroness Cairlin, I was beyond myself with grief and I could not think clearly. It does not make anything I did right, I did not even know what would happen after the deed, I only knew that Tearlach would be free from betrothal once more, and that was all that mattered to me. I poisoned my sister, and as the court rightly claims, I panicked and ran away, forgetting the vial. I ran to meet the Baroness, as was the plan, and upon my arrival, she sent outriders to fetch the body of my sister and handed the tuft of hair and the copper necklace over to me. Everything went according to plan, but then, someone retrieved Miranda at Whitebay before the outriders got to her, and from there, well, the investigators probably know more than I do." (GM: take heed that she does not mention anything about vampirism).

Silence ruled the court room for a time, everyone lost in thought, trying hard to take in all of this. Frustration grew in many minds as they were tiring of yet another testimony suggesting more investigation might be needed. The Lord Captain however, did not relent. He was not the highest judicial authority in the county for being idle or giving up easy. He turned towards Eileen.

"Would the baroness truthfully refute these claims, or explain the accusations brought forth by the defendant?"

Eileen sat comfortably in her chair, seemingly amused but all the while unshaken by Liara and her story. She had suspected this might happen and had prepared an answer.

"I must say, I am at a loss of words at the slyness and intellect of this one. She would have made a good living in the criminal underworld with the lies coming so naturally to her. I can honestly say that I do not know if I should react at all to these claims. They are far beneath me, and I should not suffer such insolence and have her hanged immediately. However, I have never treated our subjects in such a horrendous way, and so I must courteously answer these horrendous accusations." Eileen arose, golden chalice in hand, splendid and gracious at the same time, a lady of etiquette and manners. A noble lady.

"I had never met this girl before she approached me with the copper necklace and tuft of hair. I have never had any doubts that Miranda would be a good choice for my son. Yes, she lacks manners at dinner and cannot yet walk like a proper lady, but these things, a girl will learn. She is wonderful and good, intelligent and respectful to others, lords and commoners alike. Liara has said herself that which needed to be said: she poisoned her sister for purely selfish reasons. I commend her for coming up with such an amusing tale, and such a great courage as to accuse the lady of her lands, albeit rather improper and ungrateful. I have no urge to punish her harsher than the law requires, and so, leave it to the Lord Captain and other court members to deem my defence truthful or not, and judge Liara Belltower accordingly."

A second deliberation takes place without Eileen, but since the player characters did not manage to find the hidden torture chambers or bring any of the vampire's victims to court, they find Liara's story lacking of evidence and believability. She is sentenced to prolonged servitude in the Perpetual War against the blackbloods (the closest a Alerian comes to a death sentence). Ellen is freed of all charges, and Tearlach gets to marry his beloved Miranda. But Eileen and Brodan is still there, ever scheming, ever plotting for more power. See *Grey Ending* at p. 15.

Torture Cellar only (Miranda thought dead)

If the players manage to infiltrate the estate and find the second secret entrance in the master bedroom and extract the three victims found in the dungeons, they will present them to the court where all can see signs of blood loss, maltreatment, and most importantly, neck marks. If this comes to pass, there is very little left for Eileen to do but to accept defeat. She confesses to being a vampire but will take Liara with her in the fall in a fit of fury that it all was somehow her fault. She will reveal the plot and how she forced Liara into undeath, and Liara confesses, leading to her execution by Iron Ring. Eileen never mentions that Miranda is in fact not dead, and that secret will follow her into death, leading to the *Sorrowful Ending* at p. 15.

Miranda's Testimony, Torture Cellar

Eileen grudgingly realizes it was ultimately she who failed to create the perfect setting for ridding herself of Miranda, and she was to pay the ultimate price for her arrogance. In hindsight, she should have just hired a skilled assassin to rid the world of Miranda instead of being weak and wanting to spare her life, hiring instead a novice whom at least was dedicated to the cause. Formidable as she is though, she will not go down without a fight, and so, out of nowhere, she calls her guards to her side, releasing spells and curses whilst signalling to Brodan to fetch the horses to try a desperate escape towards the north, to slip out of this blasted Lord Captain's reach. She targets the most dangerous enemies with shackle spells, and those who appear weakest with damaging spells, in that order. She will be tightly guarded by four houseguards until they die or escape with her. After four battle rounds, or when there is only one guard left to protect her, she breaks away and tries to escape through a window leading to the balcony walkway. If she manages to get this far, she will climb down one of the small pillars and make a run towards the stables. She will not care saddling her stallion and breaks away with tremendous force. At the gates, she screams to the gatekeeper to open, and he complies. (GM: she will probably not get away from the court room, but if she does and manages to escape, the players will receive a -10 XP penalty for the *Righteous Ending*, letting the main antagonist escape justice.)

If the escape fails and the baroness is neutralized (<1 LP), she is detained and put in a cage for large birds (to prevent her from turning into a bat and escape). She is taken to Caislean Uisce for execution, leading to the *Righteous Ending,* p. 14.

Baron Brodan Cairlin

Age: 56
Combatant, Offensive
Vampire, Second of the Cairlin Bloodline
Allegiances: Crown of Noralac, Night Court of Wolfstone
Relations: Eileen Cairlin (wife), Tearlach Cairlin (son)
Locations: Cairlin Estate

| STR: 18 | END: 16 | DEX: 12 | SWI: 13 | INT: 10 |
| WIS: 9 | RES: 18 | CHA: 12 | AWA: 18 | |

Life Points: 108 (Vampire: when killed, the body begins normal Recovery until healed. Upon reaching maximum Life Points, the vampire rises again. Only way to kill a vampire is by banishing its soul, or binding it to an item, place or will.)

Recovery: 20 LP/day	Spell Points: 76	SP Recovery: 19	Movement: 5 meters/AP
Damage mod.: 2d4	AP: 5/BR	Fear Mod. +6	Reaction: +4
Resilience: 7			

Ceannaire Catalion (Battalion Commander). Full Heavy Armour: 5 DV. Adorned with the Cairlin crest: A round red serpent on a dark green background, and the typical green greatcloak of Broadland army officers. He wields *Briseadh Screamal* (*Screaming Vengeance*) – a large two-handed sword said to have killed a hundred blackbloods and beheaded a hundred soldiers for treason for abandoning their posts. It is decorated with golden heads of gargoyles at the hilt, and the blade is made of red iron, creating a sinister gleam in the candle-lit halls. The sword does 4d6+3 damage, and forces a fear roll on all onlookers after each kill. AP cost: 3/Attack.

Skills	Skill level
Armours: Heavy Armour	12
Arms: Two-handed Swords, Bows, Crossbows	15
Combat Tactics	12
Economy	10
Geography: Grimlake, Wayland	14
Heraldry: Alerians	16
History: Alerians, Orcs	11
Hunt	17
Laws and Rights: Broadland	11
Leadership	11
Riding: Horse	17
Society and Culture: Broadland	14

Ability: *Lead Attack*
The Baron revels in bloodshed and is the first to charge into the melee. This inspires confidence in his subjects, increasing their Damage on all attacks for the first Battle Round with +8 for heavy weapons, +4 for normal weapons, and +2 for minor weapons, as long as the Baron is heading the charge. Lead Attack only works on the first Battle Round in a battle.

2ⁿᵈ Ability: *Blood Baron*
The Baron heals for 50% of all damage done by him.

Personality

Baron Brodan Cairlin was born of Baroness Elise Cairlin - former Dame of the Knightly House of Murchaddan, fifty-six years ago. Her father was Baron Irnor Cairlin, first son of Baron Merrian Cailrin, and they were widely known for their skills in land and state management. As the young lord grew into maturity, he met the beautiful, smiling Lady Eileen Inion an Odhran at an aristocratic wedding celebration at Caislean Uisce. They fell in love, married, and governed the lands of mid-eastern Faerann Eadar as Baron and Baroness Cairlin. Until his wife journeyed north to attend her brother's funeral, everything was good and promising. But then the dark veil of Wolfstone fell over his beloved, and upon her return she did not waste many days before Brodan himself was turned into undeath. Brodan found out he did

not really mind his new-found powers, and with them, he decided to indulge himself in activities he wanted to try out for many years. It was then he became a battalion commander and honed his military and fighting skills. He ordered the forging of his great sword *Briseadh Screamal*, spending a small fortune - a quite significant part of the Cairlin treasury - on its making.

The Baron was most known from the sad fate his battalion - the 2nd Springlance, numbering seven hundred and seventy-five men and women - suffered at the battle of Rotbog, where they were surrounded and attacked by a force of orcs numbering ten times his force. The orcs made a thrust cutting Brodan's battalion in half, creating a three hundred meters deep pocket separating the front of the battalion, where Brodan and most of his officers were, and the back, commanded by a low ranking Third Leader of the Company. Seeing the overwhelming numbers of blackbloods, this officer chose to withdraw the soldiers to the east during the cover of night and linked with their sister battalion, the 3rd Springlance, instead of either holding their line or make an attempt at relieving their trapped friends. They slipped away almost unhindered, but was discovered once they were on the move, causing a surge of orcs to the area wanting a part of the action and bloodshed. Brodan believed his rear was involved in heavy fighting and thought this the only time for a push back. As demanded of broadlandish commanders, he lead the charge. The blackness of the night caused confusion, and the tide of orcs was almost impossible to punch through. With a heavy loss of life, Brodan managed to thrust through to the positions where he believed the other half of his battalion held fast, only to find the location abandoned without so much as one fallen friendly soldier to be seen. The brief stop did little to increase their chances of seeing the sunrays of the next morning, and so they had no choice but to press on towards their earlier battle lines. Once there, they found them infested with a small band of orc scavengers which they made short work of. Only there did they manage to dig in, reload the ballistae and halt their pursuers. Following morning the rear forces reunited, and it was quickly realized they had sustained minimal casualties. If they would have held their lines, the surge of orcs would not have happened, and Brodan would not have committed to a counterattack to save the soldiers in the rear. This was an act of treason according to Alerian military doctrine, resulting in the death of some staggering three hundred and sixty soldiers and officers. The punishment for treason was death, and Brodan had no trouble carrying out the sentences, seeing at what great cost the act had cost his men, but more importantly, his reputation. He decided he would personally behead a hundred traitors, including all officers, with his own sword. After two days of executions, most soldiers thought the sword's name fitting, as it had been the bane of almost a whole company of their own countrymen. Brodan deemed the executions just, but later on rumours surfaced among the men, spiritual as they were, that the souls taken by the sword somehow lingered in it or around it, forever woeful for their treason and bound to eternal unrest to wherever the carrier of the sword went. Some even said that you could hear their lament when the sword was swung.

Brodan is a typical calm, firm and harsh commander and warrior. He is logical and believes that the ends justify the means. Honour and glory is of significance, but loyalty goes above all else. Paradoxically, following his wife giving him the kiss of death, his loyalty also came to include the Night Court of Wolfstone – the instigator vampire aristocracy that embraced the first Cairlin, led by Count Iorval Wolfstone. Because of his vampirism, his loyalty was now fully dedicated to both factions, even though the human Crown of Noralac was in direct opposition to this and other rumoured echelons of organized evil, and he should only be able to choose one of the two. Somehow, he has managed to avoid loyalty clashes altogether, but will find himself in a problem caused by his wife he will have significant troubles getting his bloodline out of.

Brodan during the first trial

The Baron is the factual owner of the estate and its lands, even though he mostly leaves its management to his wife in mutual trust and respect, indulging himself in more interesting activities such as hunting animals (and human victims), archery, and political visits to other estates, burgs and castles. He behaves calm and collected during the accusations, not having to do much talking as Eileen handles that. He only reacts against the accusations of the Cairlins supposedly having hidden torture chambers.

Hidden torture cellar

Unexpectedly, the Baron leans forward threateningly, causing everyone to notice and quiet. The large man possesses a natural air of authority and power, enhanced by his gilded throne and his great weapon resting in its sheath leaning on one of the arm rests.

"You come into my lands. You come into my town. You eat my bread, you take what my son has offered you. In good faith, I let you roam my countryside in search of news as to Miranda's disappearance. And yet here you stand, accusations spewing out of your mouths like the venom of a snake with mouth agape. Why, I cannot fathom, for such is the curse of loyal men. But I know about rats. They dwell were no man of honour sets his shoe, spreading deceases from one rotten den to another, all the while not knowing the responsibility they carry. So work the minds of outlaws, of criminals, of brigands dwelling in the forests, in manure produced by themselves. Where one disillusive mind exhumes its disease, other catches on, and from there, it spreads like a plague. And so here I sit, in my own court hall, the long and glorious legacy of Cairlin slandered by persons afflicted with whatever sickness of the mind that has entrenched

itself within, like orcs having captured an alerian keep." At the mention of their atrocious enemy, a noticeable part of the court blackens in brooding hate, listening with more wilfulness to the baron's words.

"Impartial that I am, I shall not punish those before us as they are but a result of a pestilence I have left unchecked in the wilds for far too long. I will deal with them, gather the soldiers, and purge Faerann Eadar of their filth. As for these accusations, I gracefully bid the Lord Captain welcome to examine all abodes and rooms of this fair estate, to safeguard the legality of my claims. There are no hidden torture chambers in our lands. At best, these rumours may refer to the prison for witches, legally built and sadly needed in these times were personal gains seems to become ever more important than the Crown and its peers. The punishments carried out there accords to the laws, as the Lord Captain will see if he so wishes."

To this, Lord Captain Falconer shakes his head and raises a hand, already assured of Brodan's honesty.

"It will not be needed Baron. Clearly, these accusations must be misplaced as a result of lies told by the brigands of the woods. Everyone knows this in the lands of Noralac and the other realms; the men that dwell in the wilds are enemies of the crown and its people. They are criminals, rapists, murderers and traitors, and they avoid justice by hiding. I am severely disappointed by this part of your report and accusations, investigators, but I shall find the strength to look past these violations against a Lord of Broadland, and not dismiss your other, more interesting claims."

Brodan before the second trial

If the players tried accusing the Baron of housing hidden torture chambers in the estate cellar, the first thing he and Eileen does after the meeting is ordering their most faithful house guards to raze the tunnels from the barn and pack the floor so hard it is impossible to distinguish there having ever been a hole there. They keep their secret entrance in their master bedroom.

Brodan will also hire four assassins when things are starting to get out of control. They will show up sometime before the second trial decided by the GM and will have no traces on them which can track them to Brodan. As a matter of fact, the contract went through three hands before ending up at this specific guild of assassins, so even if the players would manage to beat them up, charm them or cast mind reading spells on captured assassins, they would not know more than that they got the contract from a female only known as Red Esmeralda, residing in the criminal underworld of Sandsburough in the Astweald County. Needless to say, it would simply take too much time to follow this lead, and so Brodan outplayed them in this matter. However, assuming the players survive, there is very little for Brodan to do than to await the outcomes of the second trial, as he cannot himself engage the players or their allies in any fruitful, uncompromising ways.

Brodan during the second trial

Brodan will not say much, letting his Eileen speak for him. However, he will act on her directives if things start going southwards. Before the trial, she approached him and bade him to ready their horses, in case they needed to break the pact with the crown and become residents of a new keep in the depths of Wayland. Additionally, he has prepared the outriders (those that remain) to act as their bodyguards on the journey. If Eileen orders him to make his way to the stable, he will draw his sword first and act first of all, and he will cut down John Wood being the closest to the right and performs two attacks on Ida Hayleah before heading in the direction of the balcony window. He is alone as the four house guards close enough to him and Eileen has created a human wall around Eileen, and he is thus susceptible to attacks. He will hesitate once out on the balcony, waiting for his wife, not sure if she will hold her ground alone. If the players and good npc:s manage to hinder Eileen from getting to the balcony, Brodan will thunder back, his sword poised to strike. If Eileen gets out to the balcony, he will help her down the pillar like a true gentleman and secure her escape by taking the rear guard all the way to the stables. Should they manage it this far, the players are doing a very poor job at defeating them, and they will be reinforced by 10 (- eventually killed outriders from engagements earlier in the adventure), all mounted on horseback. If they manage to fully escape, this leads to a second version of the *Righteous Ending* (p. 14). Instead of them facing justice at *Caislean Uisce* they manage to escape to the forests of the north, their brooding hate forever growing under the dark tutelage of Count Iorval Wolfstone. It would be hundreds of years, however, before they openly acted against their old homeland, trying once more to wrest control of the estate, now with an army of undead in their control.

Mordoc Whiteveil

Age: 65
Combatant, Defensive
Human, Alerian
Allegiance: Himself
Relations: None
Locations: Mordoc's "Fishing" Shack, Cairlin Estate

STR: 5	END: 4	DEX: 6	SWI: 5	INT: 18
WIS: 19	RES: 15	CHA: 7	AWA: 18	

Life Points: 58	Recovery: 10 LP/day	Spell Points: 148	SP Recovery: 37	AP: 4/BR
Movement: 2 m/AP	Fear Mod. +2	Reaction: +2	Resilience: 5	

Skills	Skill level
Banish Soul	10
Bestiology: Undead	14
Command Entity	8
Conjuration	14
Instrument: Violin	16
Languages: Tongue of Evil	6
Surgery	12

Conjuration Spells	Spell level	Page (*Vindeon – An Adventure Role-playing Game*)
Raise Skeleton	3	197
Raise Corpse	2	197

Personality

Mordoc Whiteveil is a quiet and socially awkward old man. He does not get jokes, sarcasm or irony, and takes everything literally, logically answering accordingly. He is not evil per se, but more of a neutral character with an intense interest in the necromantic arts of magic, and of the true essence of souls. He considers himself a researcher of life and death, trying to solve the many mysteries concerning the differences between necromancy, shamanism and the practices of fogwalking and witchery. Why can corpses be reanimated through the void energies of magic when forcing an existing soul into a corpse to make it a living dead does not work? And how come you can force a soul into a dead corpse by the powers of the divine – through shamanism or fogwalking? Are they not the same thing? Such questions boggle Mordoc's mind, and he has dedicated his life into doing experiments to unravel these mysteries.

Mordoc is rather polite and matter of fact, and when the players meet him he is startled, but settles down quickly once he believes they have not come to do him any harm. He travels the world, not really knowing where the road will take him since necromancy is frowned upon and he is frequently chased off from different dwellings. This abandoned fishing shack is simply his current dwelling and laboratory. He owns a donkey named Grass which he treats well, and a violin that he plays excellently, being his only real diversion from his work and surviving on his own.

Meeting Mordoc

Mordoc is not difficult in a hostile way, but he is rather secretive with his research and does not give anyone any information out of the blue. However, he is not impossible to ask, and if people treat him with respect and goodness, the chance is great he will act sincere in return. If strangers come into his abode and mistreat him or show signs of the ordinary disdain and prejudice he is used to receiving, he will not even reveal what he ate for breakfast. If the player characters are nice to him, he will answer following questions truthfully:

Miranda's body

He found the body just above the beach-line during his daily walk at *Whitebay* for gathering dry wood for fuel washed up at the shoreline. Another dead body to conduct experiments upon he thought and returned to get the donkey. Slyly,

he steered Grass to keep to the water-washed sand so that the waves would wash away the hoof marks. He managed to haul Miranda onto Grass and get her into the lower floor of the fishing shack – the floor with the hole and suspenders for lowering a small boat into the sea. He does not say more.

Rumors of witch attack

Mordoc raises an eyebrow, then shakes his head in understanding.

"See, whatever someone has told you was the cause of this girl's death, it wasn't some witch's spells." He removes the blanket over Miranda without hesitance, exposing her naked body to the embarrassed audience. (GM: Players roll against Resolve. Success: Manages to hide their embarrassment. Failure: Blushes in embarrassment). Mordoc does not understand the reactions of the others. To him, this is just a body – but one of the many he has had during his years.

"One does not have to look neither long nor closely to see that this girl does not show any signs of external damage. This means that the witch might have cast spells causing internal damage, but my examination reveals no signs of such attacks has occurred as well." He puts a pointing finger on her stomach. "Would the attacker have caused internal bleeding in her abdomen, it would show as dark areas here and here. If her heart would have been squeezed causing her death, her eyes would have been swollen as well as her lips and tongue, but as you can see" he says and opens her mouth with a peculiar metallic instrument whilst using his other hand's thumb and index finger to force open Miranda's eyelids "none of them shows such signs." He releases her mouth and eyes, and resumes a thinking posture, one hand supporting his jaw and the other that arm's elbow. Unaffected, he leaves the body uncovered to some party members dismay. He seems to be sinking into his own thoughts, not really noticing the players anymore. If they do not press him further on the matter, he will wander off to the other floor to cook some food for himself. If the players steal the corpse once he is away, he will not try and get it back, it does not matter too much that he lost it, just a little. But there are always fresh specimens at the graveyards, although most of them not being as interesting as this particular one.

The cause of death

If the players press the matter further and actually asks Mordoc what might have killed Miranda, he gives them a surprised look. Then he produces the strange mouth-opening tool again and, well, opens her mouth with it.

"Yes, I did only find one reason as to this one's condition. It seems she has gotten some poison into her digestive system." He leans forward so close to Miranda his intrusive eyes are mere inches from her mouth, looking down into it. "Her oesophagus is slightly blackened, body lax, indicating she must have been poisoned with some paralyzing agent. If I were to guess, I'd say she drank this concoction and collapsed almost immediately, seeing as she shows no signs of struggle from drawn out torments, such as bodies experience from poisons like vitriolic acid or rat poison, not to mention many venoms of spiders and serpents…" Mordoc is lost in thought for a while.

"Interestingly, she has not awoken, which would have been the case were she to have drunk the common paralyzing poison concocted by the venom of marsh toads and goblin blood. Normally, the effects last for a mere couple of hours, but it has lasted the greater part of a full day now, and she shows no signs of feeling better." There he stops, lost in thought. After a while, he starts for the upper floor, determined to cook himself some food.

Miranda is not dead

If the players remain curious and ask him what he means, is she dead or not, he sighs at the notion of continuously postponed dinner, but obliges their curiosity.

"Indeed, this body seems to rest at the brink of death, its soul verging on the chasm of souls. But she has not yet passed over and her condition has remained the same since I found her. Most interesting!" he adds, scratching his tassel of a beard. "I have not yet heard of a paralyzing agent capable of producing such helpful properties. Imagine what experiments you could conduct on sedated living samples! Surgeries requiring precise incisions for hours would be made easier due to the fact the body not waking, not struggling against the scalpels, scissors, knives, needles and other instruments needed for such important tasks!"

Unfortunately, this is where Mordoc's expertise ends, as he himself has no idea as to how to concoct such a useful paralyzing poison. If the players explain their mission, to bring this girl back to life, or at least to her betrothed in her current state, Mordoc will not protest. He already knows how steadfast people are in the protection of loved ones from experiments such as his, and he wants no quarrel with anyone, especially local lords, and so he proclaims she is free for the taking (the last statement perhaps causing more embarrassment to the party). If the players ask of him to let the body remain in the shack whilst they report to their contractor he agrees, not wanting to be hunted through the lands because of one single body, no matter how interesting.

Asking Mordoc to hide Miranda until they return from Tearlach

If the players decide it is for the best if Miranda be kept at this hidden location, Mordoc complies. He will conduct some harmless experiments on her, he adds truthfully.

Telling Mordoc they will take Miranda with them

Mordoc complies as he does not want to get into any trouble for his art. He does not even ask for compensation for hiding her from scavengers. After all, that was not the reason why he relocated Miranda and therefore no thanks were needed. He leaves Miranda and the fishing shack with Grass, heading south towards the Highland Heads, and disappears from this tale.

Mordoc's departure

Mordoc refuses to have any part in trials and testimonies, since being incognito is one of the most important things to him. Regardless of efforts, Mordoc will leave the area once he is compromised. Not that he is in a hurry, but he will not linger unnecessarily.

Ellen the Housemaid

Age: Unknown, ~16
Non-Combatant
Human, Alerian
Allegiance: Crown of Noralac
Relations: None
Location: Cairlin Estate

Personality

Ellen is a shy, quiet and caring girl in her mid-teens, not even knowing exactly how old she is herself. She was born in the streets of Usentil and dragged into an orphanage at a young age. There she remained until the mistress of the house decided she was old enough to be sold at the serf auction, at about twelve years of age. She was bought by a passing baroness and found herself serving as a housemaid to the Baroness of the Cairlin Estate in Faerann Eadar. She is very kind to her friends and always seems to find the positive in all things. Life as a housemaid can be difficult and depressing, but she manages to keep the spirit up, lifting others as she does. Everyone who knows her, being only other servants, knows that she would never hurt a fly, yet she was thrown into the prison to be tortured into confession of being a witch. If anyone would ask her serf friends, they would support her innocence stalwartly. But no one asks serfs.

Ellen before the first trial

Ellen is out of reach for the players because they are denied entry to the estate by its masters. She is tortured as a tactical move by Eileen to make her more submissive and defeated before her testimony. She endures, even though her body and spirit break a couple of times during the horrendous two days in the estate prison. Nevertheless, her sense of duty and fairness prohibits her from confessing something she did not do, even more than her will to live. She knew well what the consequences would be if she survived this and was freed of charges. The Baroness brought pain upon her with ill hidden zeal, revealing to Ellen that she had more invested into this than simply being her mistress and responsible of her servant's actions. She knew well that the punishments would continue, were she to survive. And so, a broken but determined girl is brought before the court.

Ellen during the first trial

Ellen stands as the accused, but when addressed she will honestly deny that she is both a witch and that she attacked and killed Miranda at Whitebay. She will also be true about her having no idea as to how her copper necklace and tuft of hair ended up at the crime scene, but she will be just as honest about these items belonging to her, which in itself does not help the court towards finding her innocent. But Ellen had lived a hard life and did not flinch. The only thing that really caught her off guard was the weird sensation of talking to so many high lords and ladies at the same time, moreover being the centre of attention.

Ellen before the second trial

Providing the players found enough counter-evidence to force the court to postpone the trial's verdict, Ellen is sent back to the estate prison. This time, she is treated better, as the accusers cannot presume her being neither a witch nor guilty of murder and is therefore not allowed to torture her. According to alerian law, prisoners may only be punished if evidences are true as of their crimes but they still keep lying about their innocence. The level of pain they must endure corresponds to the severity and nature of their crime. The players are allowed to see her, but she will not provide any useful information other than what she already said in the first trial. She lost her items sometime during the night when she was asleep, so she does not know who might have taken them, or why.

Ellen is executed

If Ellen is executed due to the lack of skill and determination in the players, a terrible sight will haunt their minds forever. Ellen is taken to the courtyard, in chains and crying. No one escapes the fear of death, and her face is deathly white, her body trembling. She has had time to think about the death she is about to receive, the pain, the humiliation. She could not bear the thought of her body, her identity, ending that way. She could not escape the pictures she got in her mind of seeing her own heart torn out before her eyes. She is tied hard to an angled rack, and the executioner – Lord Captain Falconer, reads the charges and the court's final verdict. A crowd is watching. Most of the estate residents have been brought out, including Ellen's best friends. They were all crying silently and they turned their heads to the ground, not

wanting to see her die this way. A mob of excited villagers from Flowerdale had gathered as well, relieved that yet another witch was brought to justice. The fire is lit in the vat and the Lord Captain does not envision a prolonged death for the girl, who he regards with pity and doubt. Looking into her eyes, he catches a glimpse of innocence and profound fear, and almost panicky, he cuts open her flesh just below the sternum and quickly severs the thick and strong arteries to the franticly pounding heart. Ellen screams in fear and anguish, body writhing in automatic reactions beyond her control. Her knuckles whiten as the wrists try to escape the ropes that wont budge, her toes wrinkling in pain. She throws her head back and looks to the sky between the tremors of her eye muscles, a plead of mercy trying to escape through biting teeth. She has unknowingly bit her tongue and inner cheek, causing blood to flow from her mouth. But she does not feel that pain. Then, as the last nerve cords and blood vessels are cut, her power diminishes rapidly. Her arms and legs stop writhing, her fingers releasing the clench. Her head falls forward, eyes faintly focused on the heart now held up in front of her. As Falconer lets it fall into the fire, Ellen's eyes shut for the final time. Her body twitches two times, and then it turns lump, unmoving. A sense of great injustice settles the courtyard like a great, crushing veil of darkness. The excitement of the villagers was gone, only an eerie silence lingering, gripping each and every one. The body still tied to the rack seemed testament to a crime now committed, and a slow fear of impending retribution came creeping to their superstitious minds. In silence, people started to hurriedly leave the place, eager to get home to their abodes, some to find solace in strong drink, others in rituals or prayers. Ellen, the orphaned girl from Usentil, who had never experienced freedom or love, had been put to death.

It is important to describe this terrible execution to make the players feel ashamed of themselves, at least if they played good characters. Also, it should evoke feelings of guilt and horror, as it is deemed they deserve this after having failed so to advance in the adventure. Results in: *Black Ending* (p.15).

Ellen is freed
Justice to varying degrees has been met. Read *Righteous Ending, Sorrowful Ending* and *Grey Ending* for each ending where Ellen is freed of the charges made against her (p.14, 15).

Lord Captain Nathair Falconer

Age: 38
Combatant, Offensive
Human, Alerian
Allegiance: Crown of Noralac
Relations: None
Location: Westgate Lodge, Cairlin Estate

STR: 16	END: 12	DEX: 17	SWI: 18	INT: 16
WIS: 14	RES: 14	CHA: 13	AWA: 10	

Life Points: 96	Recovery: 15 LP/day	Movement: 7 m/AP	Damage mod.: 1d4
AP: 7/BR	Fear Mod. +2	Reaction: +3	Resilience: 5

Lord Captain of Faerann Eadar. Full Medium Armour: 4 DV. He wears a greencloak with the knightly mark of Broadland – a tower crossed by a longsword – centred on it. Immediately under it is the Lord's crest of Caislean Uisce – a gilded ring with a crimson stone on a midnight blue background in the form of a heater shield. The Lord Captain emblem, a brass lion head holding a key in its maw, is fastened on the upper left side of his steel cuirass, and his linen garments are all in green – the eternal colour fashion of the Alerians. He is armed with a two-handed sword, 4d6+2 Damage, AP cost: 3/Attack.

Skills	Skill level
Armours: Medium Armour	15
Arms: Two-handed Swords	15
Combat Tactics	14
Geography: Grimlake, Wayland	14
Heraldry: Alerians	16
Hunt	13
Laws and Rights: Broadland	19
Leadership	12
Riding: Horse	15
Society and Culture: Broadland	18

Personality

Nathair Falconer is an intelligent man with keen senses, especially social and psychological ones. He is quick to perceive changes in tones and behaviours and is openly critical to everything he sees and hears, not taking anything for granted. This is a result of his many years as the Lord Captain of Faerann Eadar – the highest-ranking law enforcement officer within the county. As a Lord Captain, you serve as much as a detective or investigator as policing the populace, and a Lord Captain is also bound by law to perform the sentences made by themselves, if they involve executions. Thus, it is not always a glorious profession. Falconer is known for fairness and not taking anything for granted, keen on hearing all stories and versions of a case, both from accuser and accused, as well as witnesses. Most importantly, in contrast to most other Lord Captains, he is impartial to social status, and has therefore gotten a reputation of being incorruptible and unyielding to the power of aristocracy. As a result, he has become highly popular to the commoners and reversibly somewhat unpopular at the courts of lords and ladies.

The arrival of Nathair Falconer and the first trial

The players have two days prior to the arrival of Lord Captain Falconer to accumulate evidence suggesting another story being at play at Flowerdale than was first suggested by Eileen and Liara. Falconer wastes no time lingering in Flowerdale (he takes up the master suite at the most expensive inn, turning down the Baron's invitation of housing at the Cairlin Estate. He much rather wants somewhere neutral to rest, to prevent issues of indebtment to the owners of the lands.

Poison vial or torture cellar only

The Lord Captain, even though it seems suspicious that a supposed poison vial might have been on the crime scene at the time of the murder, cannot find this evidence solid enough to free Ellen of charge. The vial was found in a troll cave, and could thus, as Eileen pointed out, have been taken from anywhere in the vicinity. Nathair then has no other choice than to condemn Ellen to Witchsoul Abolishment. Accusations of Torture Cellars will not lead anywhere, as the players will be unable to provide evidence of this at court, at the same time as the owners of the estate are outraged and of course denies that there has ever been any dungeon in their estate other than the legal prison for all to see. Realizing there is no point in pursuing this even if it was true, as the perpetrators would continue to hide it from view (it is known that many keeps houses such installations for interrogation purposes), the Lord Captain has no choice but to side with the lord and lady of the house and pass judgement on Ellen.

Miranda's autopsy

If evidence suggests Miranda's body being found and showing no signs of external injuries, the Lord Captain's interest is increased. Realizing there might be more to this story than it appeared at first glance, he postpones the judgement to a second trial, demanding that Miranda be brought to the Cairlin Estate (does not matter if presumed dead or alive).

If the players have also found the poison vial, Nathair makes a mental note that this might just as well be connected to this mysterious case, but makes no presumptions in anyone's favour. If they add the supposed Torture Cellar as an additional accusation against the house, Nathair will neglect it as the other evidence are significant enough to demand more investigation and another trial.

As long as the first trial leads to a second trial, the Lord Captain will demand full access to the estate for both him and the players (investigators). The only limit being the *Master Bedroom*, which would infringe too much on the castle doctrine of alerian law.

Nathair Falconer before the second trial

Falconer is mostly unavailable during the time between the trials. He is located in the master suite of *Westgate Lodge*, the most extravagant of Flowerdale's three inns. His squire, Willir Ash, handles the "bookings" of the Lord Captain, and so, it is mostly him the players converse with. Falconer makes important notes to help in passing a just verdict in the second trial, but puts most of his time to other matters of state affairs. After all, to him this is a judicial case of minor importance.

If he is asked what they could do to make him believe in the accusations of the Cairlins housing an illegal torture cellar at their estate, Nathair simply replies that they need evidence – anything from revealing to him the actual dungeon to items such as shackles, bones or even living victims of said cellar.

Showing Nathair the *Secret Barn Entrance*

Nathair does not hesitate in deciding he wants to see this supposed secret torture cellar, and follows the players to the barn. This is done earliest during the evening after the first trial, and by then, the Cairlin House Guards have effectively razed that entrance, so when they arrive, they only see an ordinary packed dirt floor, nothing at all indicating a supposed hidden entrance. This annoys the Lord Captain to some extent seeing as he is a very busy man, but he conceals it well, and politely takes his leave back to his duties in the study at the Westgate Lodge.

Nathair during the second trial

If no new evidence is procured by the players, Nathair will need to execute Ellen. However, if the players manage to provide enough evidence tying Liara and Eileen to the crime, a number of different judgements will be passed by him. It is already described in Eileen's character reaction text at page 27-29.

Nathair leaves

Righteous Ending: Nathair takes his leave before the marriage, satisfied and highly grateful to the player characters in their instrumental work for finding out the truth, not only managing to save Miranda and convict the one who did this to her, but in the process root out two highly dangerous vampires whose terrible actions have caused much suffering and death during the years. He provides them with an *Insignia of the Just* – a brass medallion with his personal seal, which

could either serve as a medal or turned in at a guard house for three gold coins symbolizing the gratitude of the three realms.

Sorrowful Ending: Unknowing of Miranda being alive, Nathair is satisfied and grateful to the player characters in their instrumental work for finding out the truth. They managed to find out Miranda's murderess, and at the same time manage to root out three dangerous vampires: Liara, Brodan and Eileen. He rewards them with an *Insignia of Truth* – a tin medallion with his personal seal, which could either serve as a medal or turned in at a guard house for three silver coins – a symbolic sign of gratitude of the three realms.

Grey Ending: Failing in finding out the truth behind the rumours of hidden torture chambers, Nathair has no choice but to sentence Liara to prolonged service in the eternal war. He leaves for Caislean Uisce unsatisfied, with a foreboding feeling of injustice weighing heavily on his shoulders. He makes a mental note to look into this at a later time, and thanks the player characters for their invaluable help in solving the "murder mystery".

Black Ending: Even though he can see the innocence and confusion in Ellen's eyes, Nathair sentence her to death, and executes her himself. Through it all he had a sickening feeling of injustice and wondered if this were to be his first mistake in his many years as the Lord Captain of Faerann Eadar. He does not feel any gratitude needs to be shown the player characters, and so he hurriedly leaves the estate, quickly wanting to forget about this whole debacle and get away from Ellen's spirit which he had a feeling would come back to haunt him if he did not get away before it could manifest.

Supporting Characters

First Leader Ida Hayleah

Age: 40
Combatant, Offensive
Human, Alerian
Allegiance: Crown of Noralac
Locations: Ida's House, Cairlin Estate

Life Points: 80   Defence Value: 2   Attacks: 3/BR   Hit Chance: 70%
Weapons: Dual-wielded short swords, 2d6 Damage. For each Attack, off-hand weapon does [Weapon Damage]/2 Damage.

Personality

Ida Hayleah is a champion of justice and a protector of less fortunate people, such as the impoverished or the mistreated. She is summoned to the manorial court as an assisting judge, and like Nathair Falconer she is willing to accept alternative versions of the story, and goes so far as to willingly help the players by joining them in their search for the Brigand's and the Secret Barn Entrance. She does not hold nobles in high regard. In fact, she doesn't like them at all, as she has had bad experiences with them before, most cases revolving around greed, workforce exploitation and minor corruption. To summarize; she is highly helpful towards the players, especially if they seem to be honest and really want to get to the bottom of this murder case. She was a First Leader in the Perpetual War, and as all first leaders, she carries the title with her the rest of her life. During her service she did not distinguish herself remarkedly – her way of leading was mostly careful and thoroughly planned, resulting in a slower mission accomplishment rate but a higher survival rate amongst her soldiers. She did not receive any medals, but the men who served under her command will forever be grateful for getting out of the war alive so they could go back to their families and share their children's future.

Ida before the first trial

Ida knows about the Brigands and their camp, for one of her old soldiers resides within that bunch. She knows that they are not a band of cutthroats and robbers – they are more similar to a band of freedom fighters taking up arms against the rulers of the lands. It is true that the Cairlins have a strict rule forced upon the peasants and people living in the countryside, which is basically anywhere within the lands except the estate grounds and Flowerdale. It is not too harsh, but as a result of minor infringements of rights here and there, discontent has been sown in people's minds, and a few have therefore decided to take to the woods to plan for either immediate action against the lord and lady of the lands, or simply to leave. Ida Hayleah has visited her old friend at times to see how he fares, and there she has heard them talking about the Cairlins housing a dark secret, its reason for being there still being deliberated. It seems a torture chamber of some sort is present at the estate, but the "brigands" has not yet found out why it is there. Usually, rulers build them to quench unruly persons discretely such as themselves. But none of their numbers has yet disappeared, and they have not been able to reach inside the cellar to find out or who is chained within.

Therefore, Ida *searches actively for the player characters*. She will locate them on their way toward Flowerdale after their journey to *Whitebay*, which may or may not have led them to the *Troll Cave* or *Mordoc's "Fishing" Shack*. There, she presents herself and offers to show them to *Brigand Camp* because there are rumours about a darkness residing within the estate they should know of. If the players agree, she optimistically takes them to the camp where they meet the brigand leader – Ron Marston, who tells the tale of the night he and two others found the barn in the woods and investigated it. What they found was a trapdoor underneath some stacks of hay, which led several hundred meters underground before they happened upon a reinforced steel door. They were unable to force it open – it had too difficult a lock – but they could hear moans and chain rattles from within. They only went there four times, and during one of them, they could clearly hear screams of pain from inside, as if someone was being tortured in there. So far, they have been unable to open the door, but once they find someone with the right lockpicking skills, they would return and find out whatever was going on inside. Ida will accompany them to the barn if they so wish, but the result will be nothing more than additional suspicions, as they cannot get the door open before they hear guards arriving.

Ida during the first trial

Ida has a hard time believing the accusations against Ellen. Something is clearly out of order despite the strong evidence against her brought forth by Liara. She will immediately support any evidence suggesting Ellen's innocence and reasons that it is worth investigating all claims, no matter how insane they sound, before passing a final judgement. "No one wants to have the blood of innocence on their hands, right?" she asks with a challenging smile, aimed at Nathair and Eileen both.

Ida during the second trial

She will still support any claims other than Ellen being the guilty. She will not vote for her execution – she simply turns down her vote, as is allowed in alerian courts. Other than that, she will vote for all charges against Liara and/or the baron and the baroness. She will fight Eileen and Brodan and their guards if they are found guilty of vampirism and tries to escape, but she will focus on the guards as she measures herself inferior to the powers of Lord and Lady Cairlin. She might perish, but at least she knows she died for a just cause.

Genadios Agate

Age: 59
Non-Combatant
Human, Enaxian
Allegiance: The Enaxian Church
Relations: None
Location: Fionn Gaithlean

Action: Prayer to Nidesfarn: A plead to Nidesfarn to cleanse a curse from a body. Genadios always succeeds in this.

Personality

Genadios is a pious old man with a warm heart who strongly believes in the righteousness of the Sigan faith, and has taken it upon him to spread the teachings of Nidesfarn and the great gods to places haunted by darker interpretations of the truth. He is not forceful in his conviction, and not arrogant either. On the contrary, even though he firmly believes in the teachings of the Sigans, he has both self-knowledge and self-distance. He makes jokes now and then, and thinks that making fun of things in gods' creation spreads joy in the world, and thus the gods enjoy them too. He is in good health despite his old age, he has stringy muscles and a thin but energetic body. He is dressed in the white robes of Nidesfarn adorned with an embroidered sun in golden coloured silk. He is also the Temple Priest at *Fionn Gaithlean*, meaning White Spear in old alerian, a fitting name he thought since the temple was located so far away from the other more established Sigan temples southeast of Grimlake. As a Temple Priest, he is in charge of the sermons and every day life of the other priests, priestesses and clerics residing there, numbering exactly forty-seven.

Healing Miranda

Genadios does not hesitate one moment in getting Miranda healed and immediately commands two priestesses to prepare the altar inside the temple. Miranda is placed there, surrounded by incense, and as the sun strikes her body through one of the twelve holes in the roof, Genadios performs a prayer to his god, to cleanse this woman of whatever ill has befallen her, if she has an innocent soul. For he knew, as much as anything, that to so simply be granted such a great plea from Nidesfarn without really identifying the causes of the illness, the afflicted needed to be pure in soul. The light increased suddenly, basking the whole temple with its rays. Miranda seemed a conduit of pure brilliance. And thereafter the sun diminished, leaving the temple as it were. Miranda then opens her eyes, but are quickly cared for by Genadios, who tells her to rest and recover for a while, and that all will be explained to her in due time. This is a miracle, and Genadios is beyond himself with joy as his intuition about the innocence of the girl was right, and thus he believed Nidesfarn had guided him to the right decision. Miranda will rest a few hours, and either follow the player characters back to Flowerdale, or wait at Fionn Gaithlean until their return, hopefully with her Tearlach among them. Genadios resupplies each player with food for two days, and blesses them all upon their departure, adding +1 Endurance for the reminder of the adventure.

Town Reeve Thomir Belltower

Age: 54
Human, Alerian
Allegiance: Crown of Noralac
Non-Combatant
Relations: Miranda and Liara Belltower (daughters)
Locations: Flowerdale, Cairlin Estate

Personality

Thomir Belltower is a widowed town reeve with two daughters. He is calm, composed and well mannered, always helpful and tries his best to make jokes and puns, even though they are often slightly off. Nevertheless, he should be played as an inoffensive and wise man with some authority. He does not demand of anyone to call him by title, as he is of a mind that it is not title that earns respect, it is the person behind it.

The witch attack and the loss of one of his daughters caught Thomir completely off guard. As grief, anger and questions started attacking him, he entered an uncharacteristically foul and rash mood. He wanted whoever responsible for this rooted out as fast as possible. He was so happy for Miranda, and to think that she would be murdered just before the happiest day of her life… it was just too much for even a man of his patience and empathic understanding to bear. Thus, the GM should play him eager and slightly angered, even though well-mannered and as polite as a father could possibly be after the murder of his child. He will try his utmost to help the players in the investigation, but at the same time, in his clouded judgement, he is fully focused on the poor girl Ellen being the murderess, as all evidence points towards it.

Before the first trial

Ellen is in custody, evidence securely locked away at the Cairlin Estate. He went to look at them and the girl, and focused wholly on simply looking at the girl's missing hair, not the person in general. If he had, he might have noticed the fear and innocence in her, but he just asked her if the necklace was hers, and she said yes, not knowing what it had to do with anything, let alone why she was in the witch prison. Thomir promptly turned away and left her there, having answers to all he needed to know to make a just judgement at the upcoming court.

Thomir at the first trial

Thomir will not change his mind if the players approach him with evidence that might suggest another story of what happened, not before the trial at least. As new evidence is laid bare at court however, he begins to doubt the sincerity of his oldest daughter and Baroness Eileen, and thus begins to doubt his own judgement. If the poison vial and the revelation that Miranda is alive but in a coma due to the contents of the poison vial being a potent, enchanted paralyzing poison, he turns neutral. He believes the evidence against Ellen is solid, and deep inside him, he really hopes the new evidence has nothing to do with his daughter. But he cannot be certain, and fair as he has always been, he therefore votes for a continuation of the investigation. As for Miranda being alive, he immediately demands she be brought forward to him, but this is refused by Tearlach who proclaims the safety of Miranda will be at stake were he to move her into Flowerdale or the estate.

The possible accusations of the Cairlins having hidden torture chambers, Thomir simply refuses to acknowledge. He's known the good Baron and Baroness for most of his life, and never have they done anything even remotely as horrid as this. If this is the only evidence suggesting Ellen is innocent, he simply shakes his head in disbelief – even if they had dungeons it has nothing to do at all with this murder!

Before the second trial

Thomir is starting to recover from the initial denial and chock of the fact that his daughter was thought dead, but now may be alive. As a result, he will now be susceptible for alternative versions of how his daughter was murdered. As Lord Captain Nathair Falconer did not fully accept Ellen being a murderess as there where loose ends needing to be fully investigated, Thomir snapped out of his despair and realized there might be some truth in the players' presentation of evidence. Thus, he becomes more helpful towards the players, even offering them food, drink and a resupply of arrows or bolts from the town armoury, frankly nothing more than a dank cellar with seventeen one-handed swords (4d6-2

damage, 2 AP cost), four two-handed spears (2d12-2 damage, 3 AP cost), dusty bows (4d6-2 damage, 3 AP reload, 1 AP fire) and a few baskets (10d20+20) of arrows (normal damage) and bolts (normal damage) respectively. The town has never seen war, even though some of its residents have.

The second trial and possible reunion with Miranda

If the players managed to save Miranda, bringing her to the trial, Thomir will be beyond himself with joy. His trust in the players will sky-rocket, and he will believe the evidence implying the plot by Baroness Cairlin. Saddened as he is by his other daughter's role in the plot, he will simply nod at the charges against Liara, his mind once again troubled. A cruel fate, the gods and spirits had indeed bestowed upon him and his family.

First Leader John Wood

Age: 52
Combatant, Offensive
Human, Alerian
Allegiance: Crown of Noralac
Locations: John's House, Cairlin Estate

Life Points: 70	Defence Value: 2	Attacks: 2/BR	Hit Chance: 75%

Weapon: Two-handed Spear, 2d12 Damage.

First trial

John is a moody man with a sad history, in which he lost his child to a witch. This trial evokes strong feelings in him, promptly clouding his judgement. And so, he wholeheartedly swallows the story Liara produces during the first trial, and will endorse Ellen's death sentence in all circumstances. He does not believe the player characters one bit unless they actually bring the very living being of Miranda before him. He thinks this is some kind of witch conspiracy aimed at freeing Ellen from charge. The evidence is clear and there is really only one just thing to do: cut her heart out and throw it into the fire. If he is downvoted in this, resulting in the second trial, he will refuse to talk to any of the players during the time between the trials, but on the other hand, he does not actively hinder their investigation.

Second trial

If indisputable evidence points at Liara and/or Eileen and Brodan being vampires, housing hidden torture chambers to feed on the blood of their victims, the curtain of grief is lifted and he begins to see clearly. This will result in him allying himself with the players, Ida Hayleah and Nathair Falconer to prevent the Baron and Baroness from escaping. He engages their guards as well, and may fall during the ensuing melee.

First Leader Bordrin Somersburn

Age: 37
Combatant, Defensive
Human, Alerian
Allegiance: Crown of Noralac
Locations: Hare & Pheasant Inn, Cairlin Estate

Life Points: 85   Defence Value: 3   Attacks: 3/BR   Hit Chance: 70%
Weapon: Longsword, 2d6 Damage.

Personality

Bordrin is a well-fed hearty lad who owns the hamlet of Somersburn located one mile north of Caislean Uisce. As a matter of fact, he took the name after its previous master died of old age, and he simply decided to inherit the name. He enjoys gossip and small talk, but is also interested in serious questions, mainly concerning agriculture. It pains him to hear the tidings of the passing of a young maid who were to marry the baron's son, and he is not a fan of injustice, or witches for that matter. His senses are clear and an intellectual depth can be seen in his otherwise joyful eyes if looking hard enough. He is forthcoming and wants to be of whatever help he can.

First trial

Bordrin will keep a cool face throughout the trial, taking great care to puzzle all information together. If the players have been successful in obtaining either of the three main clues; the poison vial, the body of Miranda or visited the hidden torture cellar, scepticism as to Liara's tale grows stronger in Bordrin. He will only support the execution of Ellen if no new evidence is produced. Other than that, he proposes a second trial and time to investigate the new leads.

Before second trial

Bordrin appreciates the players for not jumping to any conclusions in this mystery, and helps them in what way he can. He sincerely assures them of nothing unusual going on further to the south, not in his hamlet or he would know about it. He also has a map of the whole region which he gives the players without hesitation, even though maps are highly valued items in the human lands.

Bordrin during the second trial

Bordrin never fully buys Liara's tale, and puts down his own vote if the players failed to procure more evidence against her and Eileen. Other than that, he follows Nathair Falconers responses. He will engage the estate guards if the escape attempt takes place.

Apothecary Thornrose Venoma

Age: 44
Non-combatant
Human, Alerian
Allegiance: Crown of Noralac
Location: Three Throne Thornrose

Personality

Thornrose is a crazy, cackling woman but with a good heart and a sharp intellect shining through her ordinary fits of laughter. She owns an alchemy store, selling mostly common, low-grade salves, herbs and a few potions. She does not wish for confrontations, but will say enough is enough when it's enough. She is difficult to haggle, but easy to discuss and deliberate with. She will get exited and curious if the player characters show her the empty poison vial.

The poison vial

Thornrose holds the vial against one of her windows, apparently trying to discern any colorations within the bottle.

"Interesting", she comments, and then goes into her store room to procure two glass containers. She opens one of them and a dreadful smell immediately permeates the air within the shop, forcing the few shoppers to flee the premises, leaving only the players and her in the place. It seems to be a fine yellow powder and she sprinkles just a few grains into the vial. Immediately it sizzles, and a puff of smoke escapes.

"It's a poison alright" she decides, and immediately pours two drops of liquid from the other glass container into the vial. The smoke turns orange and vanishes in an instant.

"Paralyzing poison. Made from the venom of marsh toads and the blood of goblins. And an extremely potent one at that. Whoever drank this is most likely passed away. If not, well, should be alive and kicking after around five hours." She returns the vial to the player characters. "'Tis very uncommon to come across such a perfectly distilled paralyzing poison, I'm happy to have had the opportunity to examine it. Now, was there anything else?"

Miranda still unconscious

If the players tell Thornrose the victim is still unconscious even though it was a lot more than five hours since she swallowed the poison, she eyes them suspiciously. "You mean to say the person affected by this vial is neither dead nor have woken up and recovered?" She starts pacing back and forth behind her counter, thinking. "Curious, yet mildly frustrating."

After a while she stops and lifts one finger in a victorious "ah!", and goes to the shop's finest cabinet, unlocks it and withdraws a copper rod with a forked end. She holds it in front of the vial, and it starts resonating in a low, otherworldly tone. Her silence is a testimony to the intrigue she is feeling at that moment.

"It would appear as if the vial itself has been enchanted. By magic or spirit power, I can not tell." She thinks for a moment, before drawing a conclusion. "I can think of no other conclusion than the enchantment of this bottle being the reason the affected person has not yet awakened. Ah, the things they come up with nowadays!"

Suggestions where to dispel the effect

If the players ask her for advice as how to dispel this effect from the victim, she recommends two things.

"Well the answer to that almost spells itself. You must either visit a mage, fogwalker or priest to be able to dispel the enchantment now active in the victim. My recommendation is visiting a priest. One: there is a Nidesfarn Temple not far from here which is well-established and houses several priests and priestesses. Two: Mages are expensive in comparison to priests, who are free. And three: a fogwalker is just as likely to demand for the victim's soul than to dispel it."

Directions to Nidesfarn Temple

This also serves as the answer to many commoners, as they know where the temple is. If the players ask Thornrose where this temple is, she says its name is Fionn Gaithlean, about fifteen kilometres due northwest.

Ron Marston

Age: 25
Combatant, Aggressive
Human, Alerian
Allegiance: Crown of Noralac
Location: Brigand Camp

Life Points: 95   Defence Value: 2   Attacks: 3/BR   Hit Chance: 80%
Weapons: Longsword, 2d6 Damage. Longbow, 2d6 Damage.

Personality

Ron is a Robin Hood-type character, he is a favourite amongst the people but outlawed by the authorities (Lord and Lady Cairlin). He has a bitter taste for justice against those two, as he was once an Estate Guard and bore witness to the atrocities committed there. He is the only one who knows about the exact location of the *Secret Barn Entrance*, but as long as the players make a good impression and explain their quest to him, he will help them and lead them to it. His usual mood when with his friends is merry – he is a charming man easy to like, and you get the feeling about him that he will get things done properly and with fairness.

Ron is gathering fighters in the woods who dislike the current rulers of the land and trains them in combat – in how to use bows and axes, and he is determined to attack the estate itself before autumn sets in. He is hesitant to any ideas of attacking the estate by force before his preparations are made and he has made sure all of his gals and lads have enough training to handle themselves in a real fight, not needlessly throwing away their lives no matter how good the cause. Therefore, he will turn down any proposals of openly hostile actions during the course of the adventure.

Vampire victims: Cliona, Sinead and Óinn

Ages: Cliona 19, Sinead 32, Óinn 23
Non-combatants
Humans, Alerians. Cliona and Sinead swear allegiance to the Crown of Noralac, Óinn to the Crown of Cathalon.
Locations: Hidden Torture Cellar, Cairlin Estate

The perfect victims

Brodan and Eileen have hunted innocent travellers in the woods of Faerann Eadar for years, and always do so during cloudy, starless nights to maximise subtlety. They have never caught locals, as the rumours and questions would sooner or later start to create unrest in the region. Additionally, they have taken great care to avoid merchants and craftsmen and people of the mid to upper classes as their contacts would be able, and perhaps even willing, to create search parties and investigations in the region of disappearance, much to the lord's and lady's dismay. Their victims are people of low birth, travelling on their own to find a better life elsewhere, with few attachments from whence they came, and no relations in their destination. And so it happens that three unfortunate souls now languish in the secret dungeon of the Cairlin Estate, at the mercy of the vampire rulers of the region and their corrupt estate guard.

Pain and drained life force

The blood tastes the sweetest for vampires when their victims are frightened or are suffering. Also, the blood courses faster through the veins of the distressed, making torture an extremely effective way of reaching this quality in blood. The victims are subjected to being locked up in the dank cellar. Now and then, mostly during feeding times, one of them are put on the stretching rack, hung from the ceiling in iron shackles or similar painful positions to increase blood pressure. Sometimes they are whipped or strangled, even burned with hot irons when the lord or lady feels extra luxurious. Then, the vampire sinks their teeth into them, draining them of up to one litre blood at a time, then letting them slowly recover in a state of exhaustion and delirium. So it continues for months before their bodies cease to function and they die, often as a combination of malnutrition, blood loss, weakened immune system and physical and psychological harm. In short, the Cairlin vampires are, like all other vampires, a pure form of evil.

Cliona

Cliona was born in a hamlet close to Riverwood in Marshaw – the western part of the Wayland duchy. She was the sixth child of a carpenter and tailor, and the income just was not enough to sustain her and her younger brother. She roamed the countryside for five years, taking odd jobs here and there, never managing to settle down. Her brother died of an infection after a failed boar hunt, forcing poor Cliona to push on alone. She had just turned nineteen when she was caught following a trail towards Willholm in the night by the Baron and his men.

Cliona is the youngest person in the cellar but she has been in there the longest. She has survived for a staggering nine months, much because of her young and strong body. She is now all but broken, her mind crazed, more or less welcoming the end she longs for during each torture session. When she is saved, she collapses in one of the player character's arms, fainting at the exhilarating feeling of freedom, of hope returning, of a life and a future after all, and wakes up several hours later.

She testifies against the Baron and Baroness with burning hatred, and does not shy away from intricate descriptions of the methods used on her and the other victims. She is the only one of the three who has witnessed other prisoners dying in the cellar, and she describes what happens to them. They are simply chopped up into small enough pieces to fit into baskets then taken to the estate kitchen where they are then put into the mincer. Their remains end up as pig and dog food, and if they do not believe her, she suggests the court to have a taste of the prepared dog meals now waiting in meat storage.

Cliona's story continues. Her experiences in the dungeon lead her onto a career as a monster slayer with a specialization on vampires. She continues to travel the realms of Broadland, and helps many folks with big and small monster problems alike. She finds a life companion in Harrion North, and together they create a powerful monster slaying duo, and they become famous within a mere ten years. They get two children and retire shortly after the slaying of Arch Count Ildor the Beheader, and are now enjoying a quiet and secure life as incognito huntsmen at an unknown location, to protect them from the different Night Courts they have wronged.

Sinead

Sinead was the only child of a dysfunctional relationship between a drunken dockworker and a failed scribe. She and her mother were beaten and oppressed by the father, and she had troubles finding friends, let alone love. She took to selling questionable potions and poisons and was quickly submerged into the criminal underworld. Her father was beaten to death when she was ten years old, and the only thing she felt was joy because she could sell his current stash of tobacco and alcohol for a nice price. However, she fell out of the local boss' favour and had to escape to save her life. She has since travelled from town to town, prowling the dark alleys and city slums, robbing, stealing and extorting as she went. Sinead was caught as a consequence of a tip from the Flowerdale Guard Captain (coincidentally also the Estate Guard Captain at the same time) that an unwanted person was just about to leave town. They overpowered her a mere three kilometres away from the estate in the direction of Fairwood Glen, disarmed her and threw her in shackles. Because of her rough appearance, the Baroness figured it best to break her and kill her off fast, just to prevent possible prison disruptions or other unfortunate incidents.

Sinead has only been in the torture cellars for one month, but is already tortured beyond redemption. Her wounds are grave, her loss of blood severe, and she can do naught but breathe and moan at times. She is unable to eat due to grievous wounds to her intestines and digestive system. Her right hand is missing along with an ear and an eye. Her kneecaps are crushed, her wrists blue and yellow from suspension. Whip marks are all over her body, having torn into flesh causing cutaneous bleeding and severe pain. Her body is so broken, most people with the slightest compassion will look away at the sight and feel sorry for her fate. She is brought to the trial on a stretcher, wounds bound. She can not talk, and is more or less displayed as the worst example of the baron and baroness' foul deeds.

Sinead can be saved by a successful Cure Disease action combined with either a successful Heal or Surgery action, or a successful spell in the Narëa sub branch of Elemental Air. If not healed, Sinead suffers the fate described below.

Sinead is transported with all haste towards Fionn Gaithlean to meet a healer, and her pain is lessened by apothecary Thornrose's herbs. But she never reaches the temple, and perishes during the night from blood rot. Her body was transported to the temple, where she at least was buried, blessed by the clerics of Nidesfarn in a beautiful ceremony, so her spirit could at last find the peace it had sought in all her life.

Óinn

Much like Cliona, Óinn is a person without a home, travelling from village to village in search for his place in the world. His parents died in the Perpetual War as they managed to hide their connection to each other in order to serve in the same regiment, which was prohibited to prevent exactly that; several deaths within the same family during a skirmish. The regiment sustained massive casualties as a result of scouts failing to spot a large warband of blackbloods pressing over a mountain determined impassable by the military commanders, and so, Óinn was orphaned at the age of five. He worked as an errant boy, a shop cleaner, stable boy, fisher and farmhand. He liked the last trade best, and had even worked in Rhuedi, learning from their skills.

Óinn was caught at the northern base of the Highland Heads by Eileen who simply muted and shackled him with spells and had her two closest guards throw him in her private carriage and transported back to Cairlin Estate. He has only been there for one and a half month, but has nevertheless suffered torture and the experience of being fed upon alive. His wounds are not grave and his body in good condition, but his mind has already taken a heavy toll. He is scared of his captor's fury even after being released, and is reluctantly displayed at court, but refuse to testify against the Cairlins, eyes crazed in horror looking upon them.

He will recover in time though, but carry a scar in his soul from the horrendous experience for the rest of his life. He does at last find his place in the world as a farmhand in the lands of the rhuedi, his faith in his own countrymen lost in the Cairlin Estate.

Other NPC's

Estate Guards

Alleged to the Baron and/or Baroness. They will defend the Cairlin rulers to their deaths, and most of them are aware of the hidden torture cellar, as they help the vampires hunt their victims. As always, rumours of evil attract sinister characters, and so, many in the guard enjoy their time in the service of the Cairlins. The rest are persuaded by a generous wage.

They also serve as the town patrol, so the players will not get much help from asking guards in town.

LP: 35   Attacks: 3   Hit Chance: 75 %   Melee Damage: 1d8.   Ranged Damage: 1d6.   Defence Value: 3

Riders of the House

Mounted elite guard of the Cairlins, chosen from the ordinary guards by the captain or directly by the baron. They stalk the woods and villages during the adventure and have orders to delay and disrupt the player investigation to their best abilities. It is unwise to kill them as it is illegal, and if the players fail at hiding their corpses, there is a chance they themselves will be detained and prosecuted.

LP: 45   Attacks: 3   Hit Chance: 75 %   Melee Damage: 1d8.   Ranged Damage: 1d6.   Defence Value: 4
Riding skill: 14

Trolls

There are trolls living in the woods of Faerann Eadar, and as always, they are unfriendly and avoiding towards humans. When threatened they attack, but can be talked to and reasoned with if the humans show a willingness to settle things peacefully.

In this adventure, the players might follow the troll tracks to *Troll Cave*, presumably finding the Poison Vial, an important evidence in the murder case. A troll named Shub found it at Whitebay when it was on its way to catch crabs. Though small, it was simply still shiny enough for it to put the glass vial into its pockets. Now the vial is neatly displayed in a small crevice in the troll hoard room, which honestly leaves more to ask for. Because it consists of a tunic, five shoes of different sizes and shapes, an axe head and a few skulls from boars, goats and an elk.

Meeting the Trolls

The trolls are agitated and lurches out from the depths of the cave to meet them, clubs in hand. There are three of them.
  "Why fair face here, face go!" one of them threatens, and the others growls in approval. If the players stand their ground and do not draw their weapons, behaves peacefully and tries to talk to them, they will stand down after a while, all the while tentative and nervous, easy to spring. If the players make threatening gestures or agitate them in any way, they will attack. If their health drops to dangerous levels, they will disengage and run away to regenerate, far away from the evil humans, their faith in them significantly lessened.

Asking if they were at Whitebay

The trolls scratch their heads. "What White… boo?"
  Once the players manage to explain that they mean the beach, one of them shines up.
"I crab meal there! Sea?" After its short fit of enlightenment, doubt sets in again, and it looks confused.
  Sooner or later, if the players press on their inquiry, it will become clearer and clearer that one of the trolls indeed was there at the time Miranda was attacked.

What Shub found

If the players ask the troll if it found anything at Whitebay, Shub gets excited.
  "It weird tiny tiny flask! Grab in sand. No time crab grab. No grab crab. Grab shiny!"

Its friends look confused. One of them asks:

"Shub grab crab or flask?" Shub stares blankly at its friends for a time, and then tries to remember for a while.

"Shub grab shiny flask! Crab boring. Crab ugly. Flask shiny! But small" Shub adds somewhat disappointed.

Letting the player characters have the poison vial

The players can trade the vial for something shinier, like a larger flask, a cold coin or something similar. They basically only appreciate glass, crystal and other shiny minerals, and metal objects. They can also try to fool the trolls into giving them the vial for free. Threats will not get them far.

Trolls can be read about at page 297 in the *Vindeon – an adventure role-playing game*.

Lord Captain's High Guard

These soldiers are Nathair Falconer's life guards, they are highly skilled in sword fighting and will give their lives to protect their lord. They are good and strong in their faith that order must prevail in any given situation, and will not be persuaded to doing devious or evil deeds for the player characters. In a presumed fight at court, they are the ones meant to step in and calm it, and to apprehend the ones that started it. If the adventure results in the Cairlins being found guilty of vampirism and torture, they will attempt an escape, and their Estate Guards will make up the rear defence, providing a fierce fight for them as well as the characters. The High Guard will provide a hole in the enemy ranks so that the player characters can slip through and hunt down the Cairlins, or die trying.

LP: 45   Attacks: 2   Hit Chance: 80 %   Melee Damage: 3d6.   Ranged Damage: 2d6.   Defence Value: 3

Brigands

The brigands led by Ron Marston are poor in equipment and skills but rich in spirit. They have all been wronged, or knows people who have been at least, by the nobility, be it the local lord and lady or others. They are common folk – farmers, hunters, fishermen, shopkeepers and one or two warriors that has just served in the Perpetual War. To be honest, the label put on them is really only used to deter support for them from the local populace, but still many believe they really are thieves and highwaymen. And yes, the rumours about them assaulting one or two caravans destined for wealthy traders might be true, but then again it is for a good cause! The brigands will not be hostile to the player characters if they maintain a neutral or supportive stance towards them and their coming revolt.

LP: 35   Attacks: 3   Hit Chance: 70 %   Melee Damage: 1d8.   Ranged Damage: 1d6.   Defence Value: 1

Maps and Places

Broadland – The Three Crowns

Broadland consists of three united realms – the Kingdom of Noralac (north), Midland Realm (center) and the Kingdom of Cathalon (south). The kings and queens reside in each realm's great city – Usentil, Fidh and Cathalon. The realms in their turn are divided into duchys:

Kingdom of Noralac	Midland Realm	Kingdom of Cathalon
Wayland	Maidenleigh	Fearghal
Loingseach	Aberbury	Fellgate
Greyreach	Drimlaigh	

It is in Loingseach Duchy in Noralac the adventure takes place, on the westernmost shores of Grimlake, just north of Greyreach Duchy.

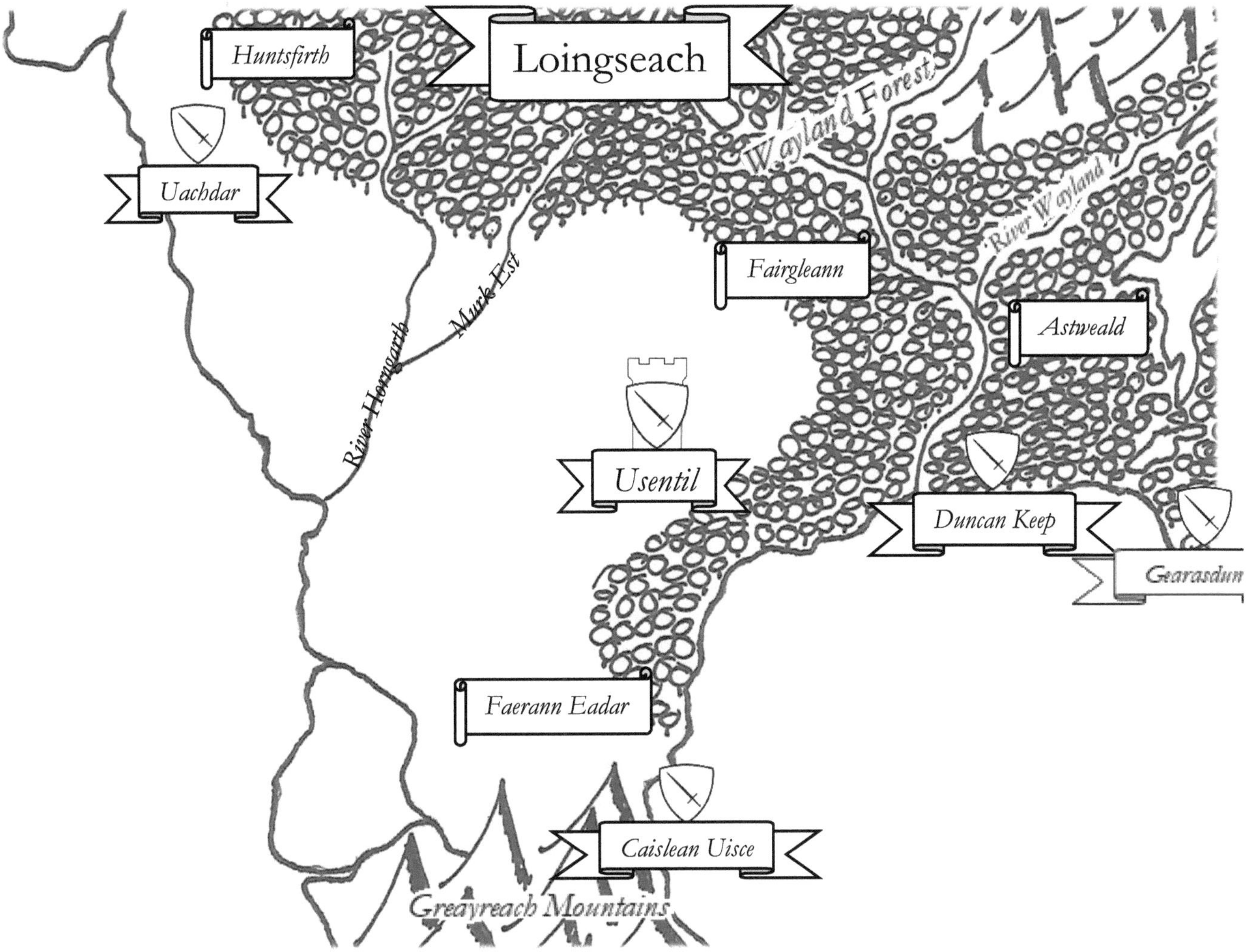

Loingseach Duchy

The Loingseach duchy is the westernmost province of all in the three realms, absorbing a good amount of the Wayland Forest in its north and eastern regions, stopping only at the stony shores of the great western ocean. Usentil is situated in Loingseach – the capital city of the Crown of Noralac and home to many noble families, among them the royal family and the nobles who owns the dukedom. The province prospers from hunting, fishing and its many lumber mills eating their way into the seemingly endless Wayland Forest. Trade is abundant as the province has many ports both going into the huge Grimlake basin and the western ocean. Most trade is done with the other realms of Broadland, as the western sea is highly dangerous to travel, not only for the orc-infested islands to the north, but also because of the shallow and deceitful waters of sharp rock formations just above, or worse, below the surface. The summers are warm and winters rarely reach freezing temperatures. But many coast-dwellers have to live with the recurrent strong winds and gales hitting the lands both from the western sea but from Grimlake as well.

It is in the county of Faerann Eadar in the province of Loingseach the adventure takes place, in its south-eastern region which houses the count's hold and its city – Caislean Uisce, as well as the fair town of Flowerdale which the plot is centred on.

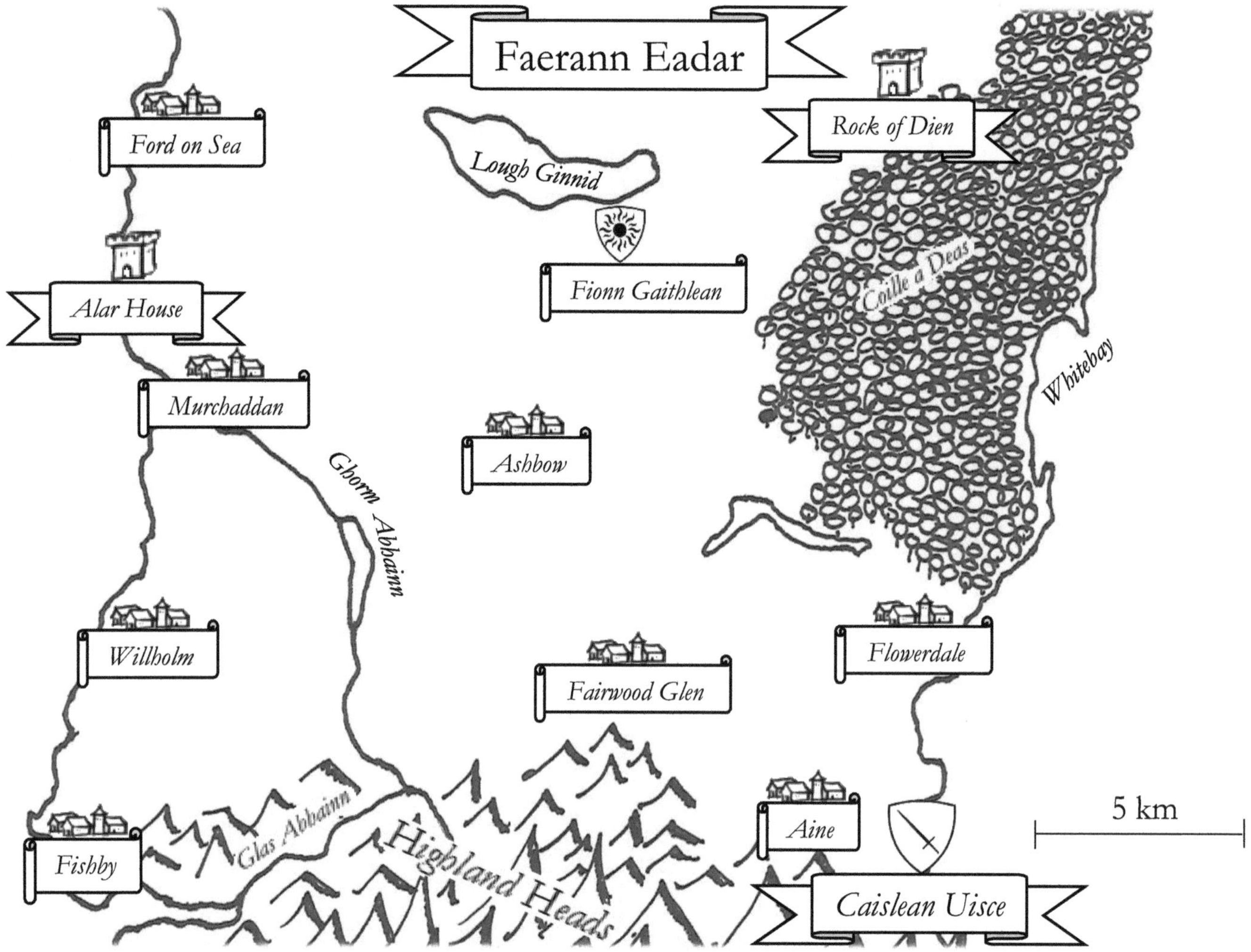

Faerann Eadar

Much like the rest of the Loingseach province, the settlers of Faerann Eadar live in harmony in their small hamlets and towns, making a living from fishing, hunting and domestic craftsmanship. The county is hilly in the north, successively getting more and more mountainous until you hit the highlands of the Greyreach Mountains to the very south. The towns are small and homely, and are seeing a small share of travellers from near and far, but most of them are Alerians. The castle town of Caislean Uisce houses the count and countess and the current soldiers of the 2nd Murchaddan Regiment currently in training for the front at Harg. Not too far north lies the blissful town of Flowerdale, on the outskirts of Coille a Deas, the southernmost tip of the great Wayland Forest, where a large part of the adventure takes place. The Cairlin Estate is located a mere half a mile away from the town. This map can be purchased from the market or the general store in any of the settlements on the map, but you do not need a map to get from town to town; roads wiggle their way to and from every settlement, littered with road signs, making travelling easy for all. Travelling the woods or away from the country roads will be trickier, even though the clearly visible Highland Heads in the souths helps a lot with orientation. The two knightly castles (Rock of Dien and Alar House) are off limits to visitors without appointment. Fionn Gaithlean is the Sigan temple near Lough Ginnid where Miranda might be dispelled and healed, and approximately seven kilometres north of Flowerdale lies Whitebay; the place where Miranda is assaulted by Liara and where the players should start their investigation. Mordoc's "Fishing" Shack is located in the southern area of Whitebay, and the Troll Cave lies three kilometres due west from the crime scene. Brigand Camp is located half way between Rock of Dien and Whitebay.

Flowerdale

Flowerdale has already been described, so this section will only list a number of points of interest, such as vendors, the town hall and the inns.

Town Hall

At the centre of town, the town hall stands as a testament to order and community. This is where the villagers gather for important discussions and meetings, and officials reaches agreements on the management of the town and its lands. Even though the Cairlins own the lands, it is the town reeve Thomir Belltower and other officials appointed by the people, who runs the everyday business and make sure everything works as supposed. The players will probably find the town reeve in the town hall on working hours.

Hare & Pheasant Inn

This inn is the commoner's choice – a cosy place of medium size meant as meeting and relaxation place for locals and travellers alike. Uncommonly, it has three floors and is therefore one of the taller buildings in Flowerdale. The main floor has a capacity of fifty guests, and serves food and drink common to the area.

Menu	Cost (Gold)	Menu	Cost (Gold)
Cheap Meal	0.03	Good Meal	0.06
Root-crop Stew	0.03	Potatoes and Pork	0.06
Pan-Fried Apples and Mustard Venison	0.06	Rum and Walnut Boar	0.06
Raspberry Tart	0.06	Cooked Egg with Bacon	0.03
Dry-roasted Apricots and Honey Mutton	0.12	Cottage Pie	0.06
Liver and Onion	0.03	Ploughman's Lunch	0.03
Steak and Kidney Pudding	0.03	Roast Lamb with Mint Sauce	0.03
Milk	0.01	Apple Juice	0.01
Tea	0.01	Liquor	0.12
Uisce Bae (Broadland Whisky)	0.14	Wheat Beer	0.03

The second-floor houses sleeping quarters that people can rent for as many nights as they want as long as they pay. A one-man room costs 5 coppers per night, a two-man room costs 8 coppers and a four-man room costs 10 coppers. The third floor is exclusively reserved for Alerian officials, and also houses the innkeeper's private quarters. It is safe to presume that he keeps all his personal belongings there. Bordrin Somersburn resides in one of the two official suites during the adventure, and can be found there, on the market, or simply two floors below in the bar, making himself comfortable with the innkeeper and his workers.

The innkeeper is Torion, who loves his occupation. He loves gossip, beer and food, and being the supervisor of an alerian inn, he can do all these things simultaneously! As a result, he is quite fat and red cheeked, and slightly greasy. He will happily answer any questions about the lay of the land, directions in town and local officials. He is a neutral character who does not care about politics or philosophy, but he is indeed disheartened when hearing about Miranda's fate. He will offer the player characters free staying at his inn, if they are indeed working for Tearlach to solve the murder case.

He has four waiters and three barmaids of young adult ages. The waiters are Lorcan, Niall, Rian and Declan, and the barmaids are Avril, Cait and Máire, all very polite and nice to people. Usually, they are serving five to ten people per evening, but during the three days of weekend, the inn is brimming with guests and it gets hectic. The player characters start the adventure on such an evening.

Three Throne Thornrose

Apothecary Thornrose Venoma's alchemy shop, named thus because its proprietor has had businesses throughout the three kingdoms of Broadland. It's located near the town hall next to the general store and the market square on the street, and there the players find both Thornrose and her wares. It is cramped with weird ingredients, flasks of conserved… things, and a different smell meets your nostrils every time you enter the shop.

Ingredients (Gold)	Cost (Gold)	Ingredients	Cost (Gold)
Agrimony	2	Aloe Vera	1.5
Blackberry	0.2	Blackfrog Venom	5
Bonemeal	0.6	Briarthorn	1.1
Oil	0.1	Olive Oil	0.1
Rapeseed Oil	0.1	Reed Leaves	0.3
Red Poppy	1.1	Red-speckled Frog	3.4
Strychnine	2.8	Sugar	0.1
Tobacco	0.3	Tulips	0.3
Virgin's Marsh Platter	2.2	Vitriol	5

Potions/Poisons	Level	Cost (Gold)
Healing Potion (10 cl)	2	2
Glowlight (20cl)	1	0.5
Glue (20cl)	3	0.3
Muscle's Warmth (5 cl)	2	0.9
Smoke Bomb (40 cl)	2	0.16
Restorative Salve (30 cl)	3	1.2
Elfstep (5 cl)	1	0.3
Oil of Vitriol (20 cl)	1	0.2
Emerald Escape (1 dose)	1	0.8
Mistralis (5 cl)	2	0.06
Nagorath (10 cl)	3	0.5
Rat Poison (50 grams)	2	0.05
Trollmind (5 cl)	1	0.8

All effects can be read in *Vindeon – An Adventure Role-playing Game* in the chapter *Alchemical Concoctions* p. 258.

General Store

The general store is a spacious building on the main street in the market square. It is owned by a woman named Muireann who is kind but unwavering when it comes to haggling or thieving. Like so many more, she has served in the Perpetual War, but managed to survive her service to the throne. She keeps her fighting skills honed and her trusted longsword beneath the counter, just in case really. She has not to this day had to use it, not even threateningly. She does not sell any weapons or armours. In fact, no one does in this town! But, should the players state their business and that they could really use some protection, she will offer to loan them her own Full Light Armour gear. Will fit a normally built woman give or take some.

Type	Material	Cost (Gold Coins)
Cap, Hat, Hood,	Linen	0.2
Headband, Veil	Wool	0.3
Tunic, Shirt, Surcoat,	Linen	0.4
Kirtle, Gown, Coat,	Wool	0.6
Cape, Mantle	Cotton	0.8
Belt, Girdle, Buckle	Linen	0.1
	Wool	0.2
	Cotton	0.2
Pants, Trousers,	Linen	0.3
Leggings, Breeches, Skirt	Wool	0.4
Pants	Cotton	0.4
Gloves	Yarn	0.2
	Leather & Fur	1
Boots, Shoes	Leather & Fur	3

Item	Cost (Gold Coins)	Item	Cost (Gold Coins)
1-man tent	0.6	2-man tent	0.7
4-man tent	0.8	8-man tent	1
Cooking pot	0.3	Cooking rack	0.6
Spoon, knife and fork	0.04	Flint and tinder	0.04
Iron plate	0.09	Wooden plate	0.02
Iron mug	0.06	Wooden mug	0.02
Water pouch	0.16	Backpack	0.2
Climbing rope/10m	0.2	Grappling hook	0.35
Shovel	0.05	Pickaxe	0.3
Sleeping Bag	0.4	Sheepskin	0.3
Parchment	0.04	Ink & Quill	0.04
Leather-bound book	0.5	Pencil set	0.05
Coal stick	0.006		
Fletcher's tools	1	Leatherworker's tools	2
First Aid Kit	0.5	Carpenter's tools	2

Westgate Lodge

Named after the ancient, ruined west gate of Flowerdale from the days of great strife when the Alerians had to flee from their mountain towns west of Harg and first settled the region of Faerann Eadar, the Westgate Lodge stands as a reminder to never take anything for granted. Supposedly, the old and almost wholly corroded iron shield that is displayed over the main fireplace was from that time, wielded by the man who would become the inn's first keeper. Westgate Lodge is a bit more luxurious than the Hare & Pheasant, and here you would normally find any delegates or traders of higher standing that happen to pass through Flowerdale to more important parts of the realm, such as Usentil and Caislean Uisce. They serve the same dishes as the Hare & Pheasant, but they do it so much better! It tastes really good, and they have some more extravagant wine, but it also costs twice as much. The Westgate has its tables more scarcely placed, and its walls are adorned with paintings of noble lords and ladies. This inn is simply more refined and exclusive. Still though, its owner and workforce are down to earth and polite no matter who comes in, and they will serve without question anyone as long as they pay and behave. They do have two guards, but they seem nice enough.

Innkeepers of Westgate is the Moore family of aunt Viola, grandma Orla, husband Willoinn, wife Seersha and five children Sheena, Bill, Iondir, Anina and Ferdran. It tends to get very "familiar" at times, as the Moores do not always agree with each other, but it adds flare and colour to the otherwise very tidy inn. The Moores do not live at the Inn, but in a larger house near the town centre, next to the Belltower residence. Its upper floor is left for the esteemed guests wishing to spend their night in Flowerdale. This is where Lord Captain Nathair Falconer sets up his private quarters for the entirety of the adventure. He can be found here if the player characters want to talk to him about their progress.

Belltower Residence

The house of the Belltower family. Miranda's room can be accessed if the players ask Thomir for permission, but there is nothing special or incriminating to be found there. It looks like an ordinary girl's room, with the exception of a beautiful wedding dress stealing all the light in the room.

Liara's room is ordinary as well, and there is no evidence pointing towards her being anything else than a poor witness to her sister's death. Liara can be found here, but she does not really want to have conversations in her room, and decides to meet them in the dining area of the house instead each time they visit.

Thomir Belltower has his private working area where at least one library's worth of papers are stored in over-stuffed shelves and the working table. Most of it is uninteresting numbers and protocols, but in the shelves there is a ledger named *List of Witch Trials and their Verdicts* containing all of the town's witch trials over the past hundred years. As they read, it seems it has been a significant increase in the trials over the last fifteen years, and that the accused have been subjected to various degrees of torture, all according to law. It seems a larger part of the accused has withheld innocence until the very end in spite of the suffering inflicted on them. (GM: naturally, the increase was caused by the Baroness becoming a vampire, setting in motion this whole horrid business.)

Whitebay

Whitebay is located approximately seven kilometres north of Flowerdale, and is easily visited due to the beautiful coast trail winding its way through the outskirts of Coille a Deas and the stormy rocks and sandy beaches of western Grimlake. Whitebay itself is sheltered and its waters usually calmer due to the natural foreland jutting out in the north and south of the bay. Whitebay consists of a long sandy beach with shallow water, making it unlikely for someone to successfully drown anyone there (if not drugged or rendered helpless in other ways.)

On the scene, tumult can clearly be seen in the sand in the form of impressions and footprints. Even hoofprints are present, and it seems the area has seen a lot of activity following the heinous crime. Miranda's body is of course nowhere to be found. The players may describe to the GM what they are looking for. If they are examining the footprints, they will be able to make out footprints of humans and, interestingly, something larger leading into the forest darkness. Someone with the skills *Bestiology: Trolls* and/or *Flora and Fauna: Wayland* might do a skill check to see if they recognize that those are troll footprints common to the woods in these parts. If successful, they can follow the tracks to *Troll Cave* if they want. If they fail, they will need the help of someone skilled at tracking, such as Ida Hayleah or her friend, the brigand leader Ron Marston.

Mordoc the Necromancer transported Miranda's body by steering his donkey through the shallows all the way back to the fishing shack, so if the players are alert, they might notice clove tracks leading down to the sea and then vanishing in the water. Also, a small shack or building of some sort can be barely seen to the very south of the bay, where the beach gives way to the rocky shores common in the area. A successful *Awareness* throw is needed to detect this. However, if the players decide to scout Whitebay in its entirety, they will discover the fishing shack when they near the southern end of the bay.

Mordoc's "Fishing" Shack

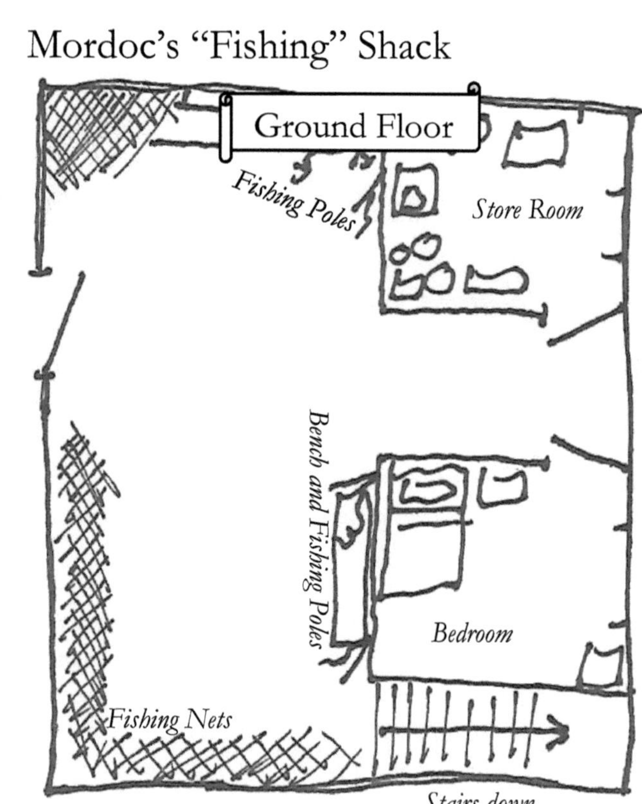

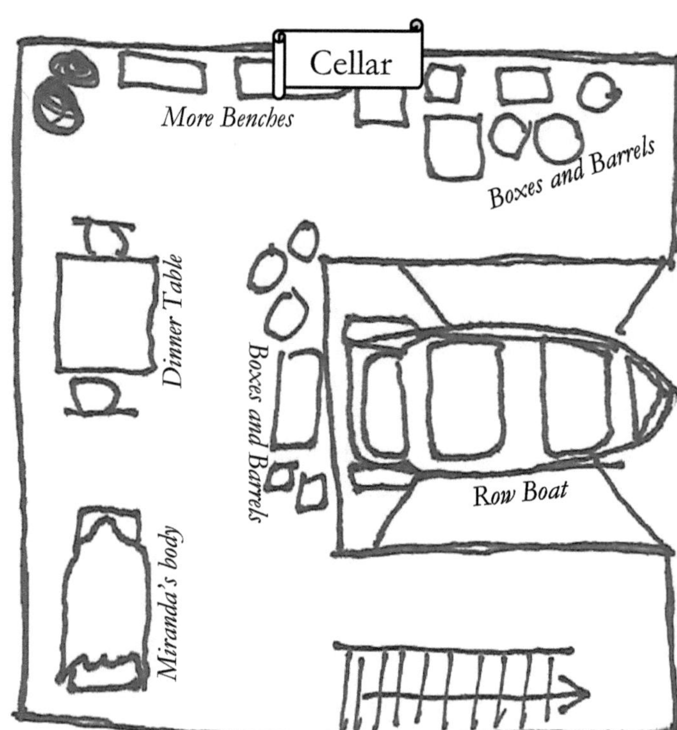

Mordoc's "Fishing" Shack is his current base of operations, but truth be told, he is not having much luck with finding good specimens. As a gift from the shadowrealm, Miranda's body appears, apparently in some kind of coma from a poison or spell. This excites Mordoc, who prepares for some experiments on her.

The shack is just that – nothing special whatsoever, just a dull, fish-catching oriented shack full of fishing equipment and empty storage containers. Whoever owned this before Mordoc clearly packed all their valuables and left the shack to its fate. At least the row boat is still there, might fetch some gold coins worth of price at Caislean Uisce, given someone has the time and energy to row all the way down there. Some dried seafood is stored in the box closest to the dinner table belonging to Mordoc, but can of course be stolen by less charitable persons. It is enough to sustain a human for ten days.

Troll Cave

Home of the three trolls Shub, Trub and Vincent, a few piles of manure, skeletal left-overs and some shoes and clothes from unfortunate travellers. They are not the best of trolls, and have merely managed to hoard five copper coins and a silver coin cut in half over the course of the years they have holed up in the cave. Shub's latest find though has added significantly to its allure, and it is now towering (with its astounding two inches height) behind the small pile of coins. The cave is small and otherwise uninteresting. No hidden doorways to goblin kingdoms or guard monsters and treasure chests. Additionally, it is rather dank and cold in there and smells of a mix between methane gas and brimstone, as is usual in troll caves.

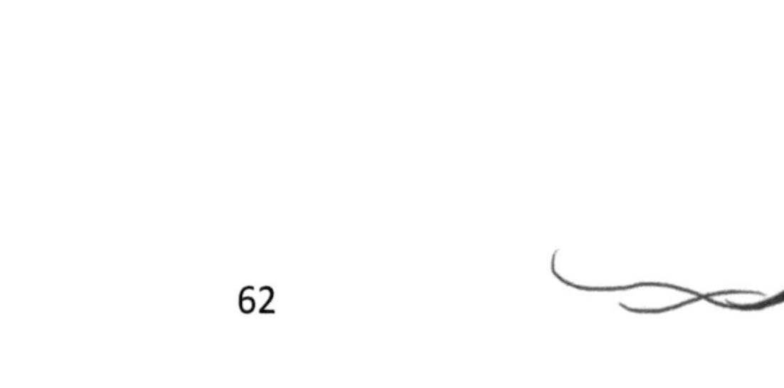

Brigand Camp

The Brigand Camp is located in a small crevice between two sharp hills, on a plateau of sorts. A waterfall pours down the mountainside and its river flows right past the encampment, and the terrain in general is rough, making it one of many good spots in Coille a Deas to hide to avoid unwanted attention. Ron Marston resides in the command tent when he is not out training the men and women for the coming revolt against the Cairlins. The camp as a whole house around thirty "brigands", but they come and go to maintain their other occupations so one can safely assume that the actual number of willing souls is double than what is present at the time. There are two entry points to the camp: the "Clearing" (bottom of the picture) and the "Bridge". They are guarded by two brigands each, who will detect anyone that is not skilled enough to sneak around them.

It is next to impossible to locate the camp, as the rebels hide their tracks excellently. If not by lucky chance, the only one who can lead the players there is Ida Hayleah.

Cairlin Estate

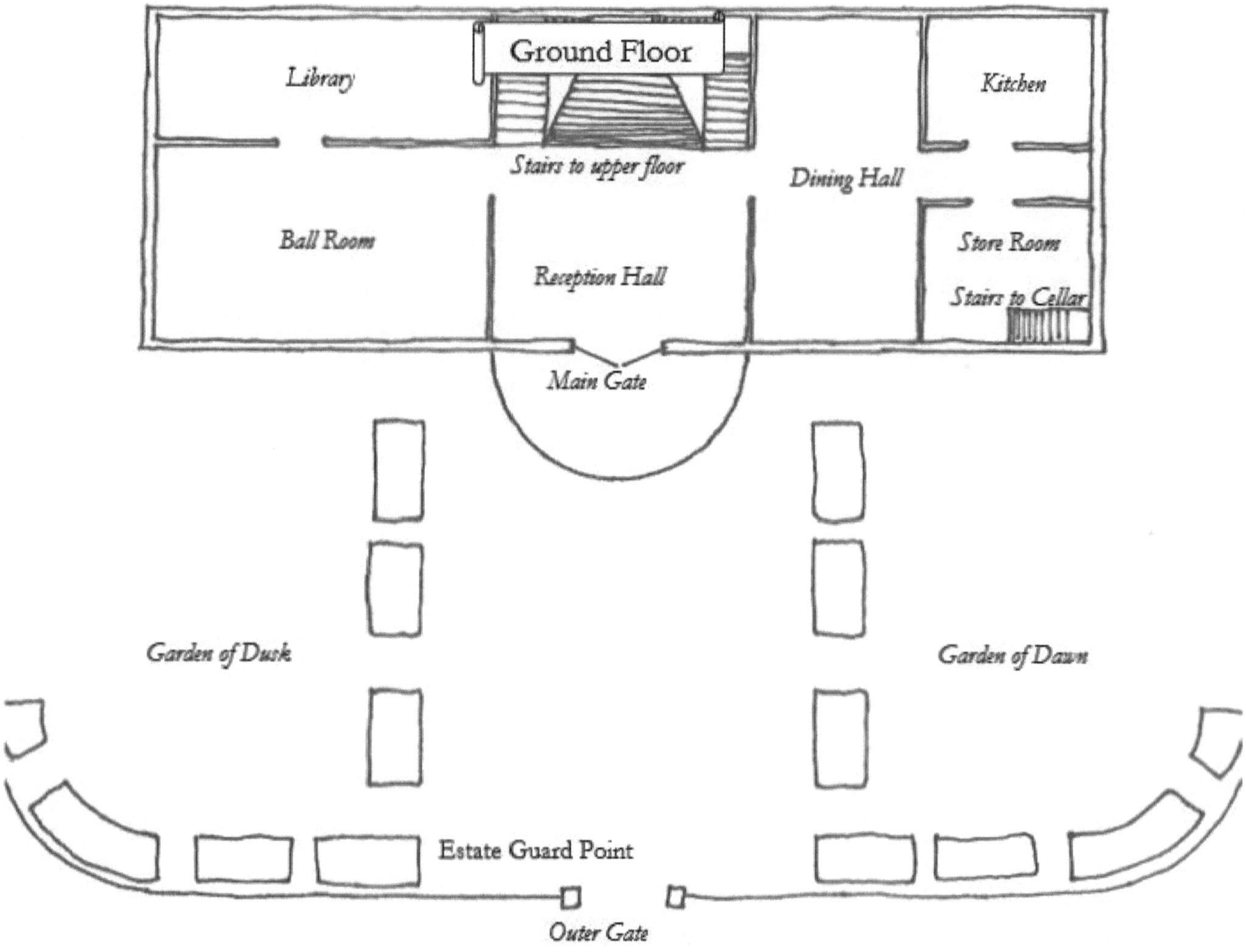

The Cairlin Estate is an imposing building, clearly reflecting the wealth and social standing befalling the Lord and Lady of the house. It is a two-floor building with a large basement. The ground floor houses a library full of books of all kinds and subjects, but notably, the shelves are arranged in such a way as to give room behind them for the secret passage down to the *Hidden Torture Cellar*, accessed via the master bedroom on the second floor. The shelves arranged this way is located on the top left corner of the library. There are a few tables for study.

The Ball Room is a very large hall for grander events such as marriage, festivals and, naturally, magnificent balls. It is exquisitely decorated with paintings depicting imposing mountain strongholds (romantic interpretations of the holds of old), wonderful landscapes and also animals common to the region in beautiful landscape settings. The windows are especially large here and the long satin curtains flank each and every one, shining with green and red colours when hit by the sun's rays. There are ceiling decorations as well, depicting a great battle, but without any fighting visible, only the Alerian soldiers charging are represented.

The Reception Hall has a green and red carpet going straight up the stairs to the second floor and both left and right into the ball room and dining room. Statues of knights are lined along the walls on each side of the entrance, and small braziers burn in front of them after sundown. There is always at least one steward here to receive guests, and on more special occasions, such as a manorial court, the lord and lady themselves greet their guests here.

The Dining Hall has a great long-table wide enough for the lord and lady to sit next to each other, and it has seats for another sixty guests. The dinner table is always set with fine cutlery of purest silver, and on the walls, the Cairlin ancestors watches over their descendants with serious demeanours, seemingly getting gloomier for each passing moon. Chances are not high the player characters will ever get invited to a banquet at the Cairlin Estate.

The Kitchen and Store Room are ordinary rooms with stored food and kitchen equipment. Two chefs charge over the cooking and has a handful of servants at their side. There are stairs leading down to the basement, where wares are stored which needs to be in cooler climate. It also leads to the official dungeon.

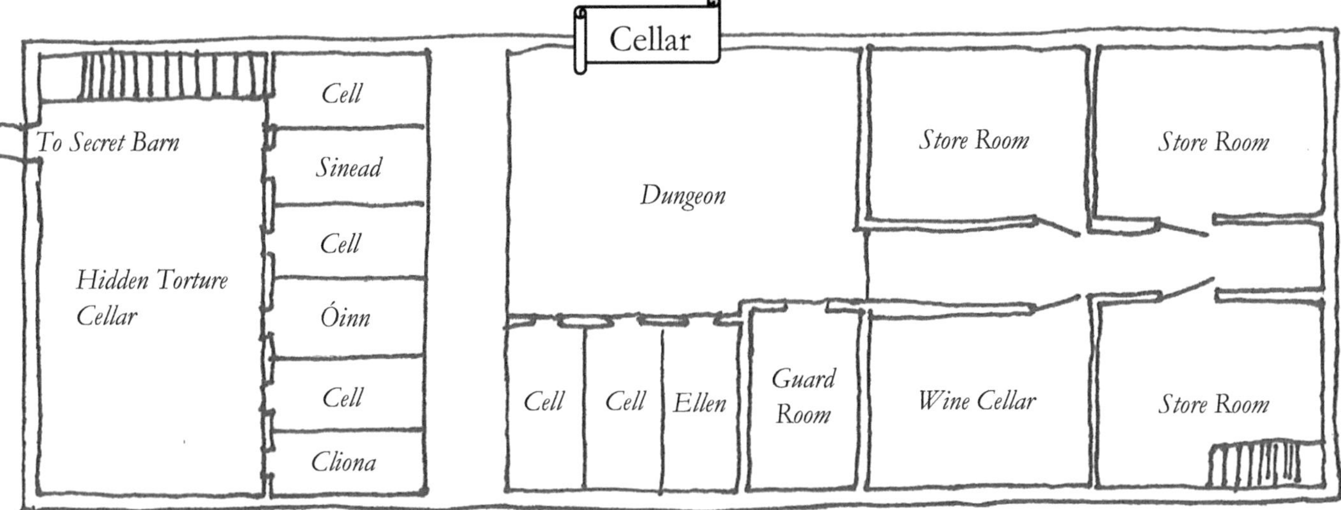

The basement level of Cairlin Estate houses its sinister truths and its double hypocrisy. For not only do they capture innocent travellers to feed upon in the Hidden Torture Cellar, they also frame innocent people for being responsible of the disappearances, accusing them of witchcraft and other crimes such as murder-robbery or manslaughter. In common for all the victims is that they languish in the dank and cold beneath the Cairlin Estate until death takes them, be it from torture, the executioner's sword or the relentless, searing fires of "justice".

The only way to gain access to the Hidden Torture Cellar is through the long and winding tunnel leading to and from the Secret Barn Entrance, or through the secret trapdoor in the Master Bedroom on the second floor of the estate. The door to the Secret Barn Entrance is a reinforced steel door which cannot be forced open unless a character has a strength of 18+, and even then, this character needs a robust crowbar to destroy the locking mechanism. The door hinges are on the inside, and if someone would be foolish enough as to attempt to blast it open with blacksand or spells, the tunnel will be the first thing to collapse. The key to this door is kept hidden away at the bottom of a flowerpot of nightshades at the window closest to the bed in the Master Bedroom, and the only time the Cairlins carry it is when they are bringing in a new victim via the Secret Barn Entrance. The lock can be picked with a successful *Lockpicking* skill roll. *The first time the player characters visit this door, they will hear guards arriving and know that they will have a fight on their hands if they open the door.*

The doors to the cells are solid doors that are locked with simple locking mechanisms on the outside (similar to those of modern-day containers). And so, they can be easily opened without keys, but are impossible to open from inside. Which cells the three vampire victims are in is displayed above. To make matters even more hopeless, they have been chained to the inner wall with short chains locking arms, feet and even neck to it, making it impossible for them to even reach as far as the door. Hay is scarcely strewn across the cells, buckets serving as latrines are placed within reach of the chained victims, but other than that, nothing more can be seen except dried blood pools and rat carcasses. The chains, like the doors, are locked with a mechanism that is easy to unlock if only you would be able to reach them with your hands. But the way they are chained up, this is impossible.

The large room outside the cells is the torture room where the vampires bring their victims when its time to feed. There is a number of infernal contraptions designed to maximise pain and suffering littering the room, a stretching rack is centred in the room, seeming to be the main method of bringing agony onto the victims.

The Hidden Torture Cellar is unmanned other than during feeding times, making it possible to free the victims unnoticed. However, once the masters of the house get a whim that the cellar has been compromised, (such as a broken lock at the barn, or a guard spotting them), they will order the immediate collapse of the secret tunnel all the way to the barn.

The Cairlin Dungeon is similar to their Hidden Torture Cellar, there are cells and methods of squeezing confessions out of the accused, but even so, this dungeon is more humane. There are four guards constantly on duty, keeping the keys to the barred dungeon entrance and the cells in the guard room. There is always one guard just inside the barred entrance

and the other three usually bide their time inside the Guard Room. Times when the barred entrance is opened is during guard change, feeding times and when visitors have come to inspect the dungeon and its inmates. You must be pre-registered in the dungeon ledger to be let past by the guards, the only ones relieved of this requirement are Lord and Lady Cairlin and Tearlach, as well as persons of higher judicial standing, such as Lord Captain Nathair Falconer.

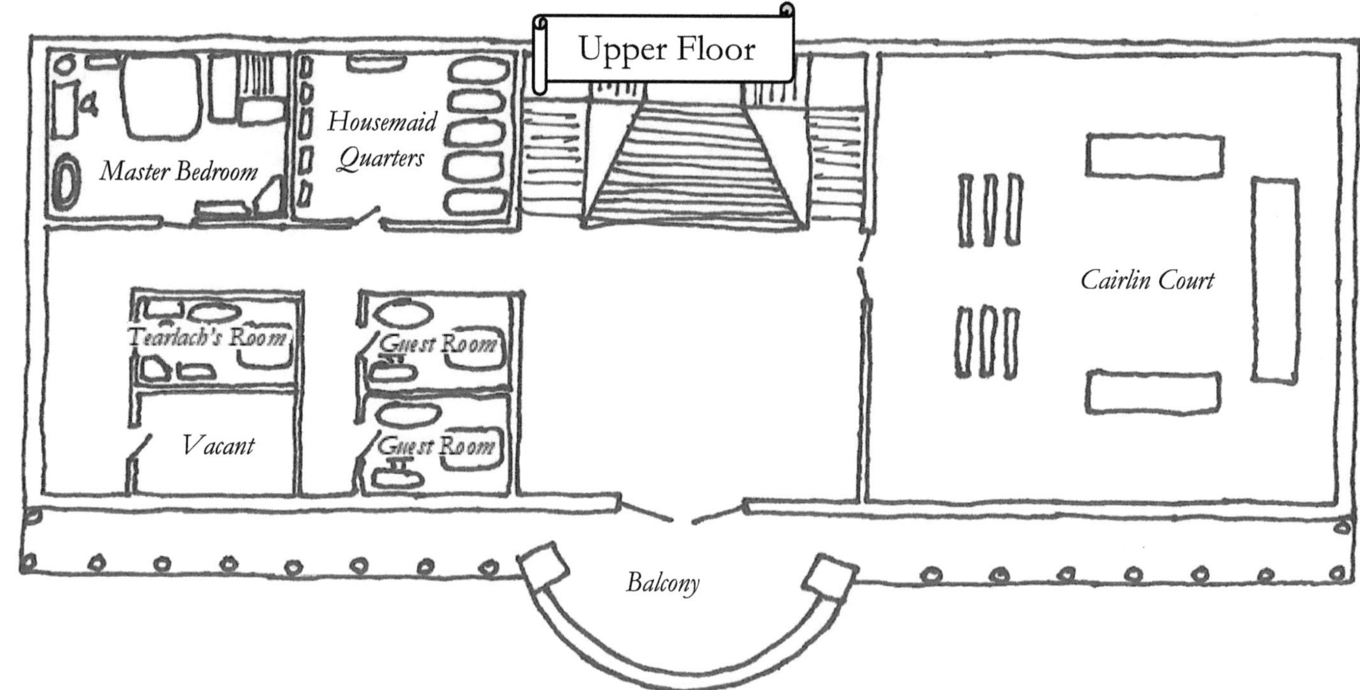

The upper floor of the Cairlin Estate houses the sleeping quarters of the Cairlins and their closest servants, as well as the Cairlin Court, where the two trials will take place. There is nothing special or secret about the rooms save the Master Bedroom which houses the undisclosed accessway to the Hidden Torture Cellar. There is a locking mechanism in the smaller of the two bookshelves that appears as a blue book with the title *War of Fear, Book III*. Unfortunately, its is well blended with its surroundings, the other seven books of the *War of Fear* neatly arranged accordingly, all in blue styles. However, the same mechanism is used quite frequently, so a thief should at least be able to know that if there is something behind the shelf, the opening mechanism usually is placed within comfortable reach of someone's hands. If a player character passes a successful *Criminal Underworld* skill roll, they will realize that this weird organisation of shelves definitely has something to hide, as they are protruded away from the corner of the room instead of aligned with it. The bookshelf door will unlock if you push the *War of Fear, Book III* two inches into the shelf. This room is not guarded, other than when a guard passes it on a regular, hourly round.

The key to the reinforced steel door at the Hidden Torture Cellar is hidden in a flower pot of nightshades, between the bed and the closest bookshelf.

The rooms of the upper floors show wealth and splendour, meaning there are a lot of fine furniture and expensive items littering tables, shelves and cupboards. Four (out of the ordinary five) housemaids scurry about tending to the lady and the house as a whole, and they are even more present than the guards. If they catch anyone sneaking around they will immediately alert the guards and the Cairlins. The Baron and Baroness have no treasure chests, as their wealth lies in the produce of the lands and the properties within. They carry all their coins on them, and the rest of their wealth (700 gold coins worth of gold bars) they have safely stored away in the castle vaults of their benefactor at Caislean Uisce.

The court room is arranged according to alerian law, with the main judges seated at the longest table at the far end of the court entrance. This is where Baron and Baroness Cairlin sits together with Lord Captain Falconer, Lord Tearlach, Town Reeve Belltower and First Leader Hayleah, First Leader Somersburn and First Leader Wood. The accused will retire behind the table to the left of the court judges from their point of view, and the accusers may be seated to the right of them. Onlookers and witnesses are seated on bench rows opposite to the court, and it is here the player characters will sit during the hearings. Every time a witness or investigator is given the word, they must rise and place themselves at the centre of the room. Once judgement is passed, the accused must stand at the centre of the room to receive their verdict.

Should Brodan and Eileen be found guilty of the murders, they will escape through the southeasternmost window out to the balcony, to climb down one of the beams and rush to the stables to get away. The Estate Guards present a solid wall of defence for them, but with the combined force of Lord Captain Falconer, his High Guard and the player characters, they will be able to punch a hole through, presenting a chance for the player characters to pursue the vampires to the stables.

Secret Barn Entrance

The Barn is located several hundred meters away from the estate in a natural ravine. It is locked with an old lock and accessible via its loft, which only requires some climbing or someone bringing a ladder. At first glance it looks like an ordinary storehouse for grain and hay. However, if you search actively for a supposed trapdoor in the floor, it is rather easy to spot. It is located far into the barn behind some hay-bale staples, only covered with some strays. Naturally, it is locked, but it can be picked or forced open. If however, the player characters leaves anything out of order, the guards will find out and receive orders to level the whole tunnel and replace the trapdoor with ordinary planks. The only ones who knows about this secret entrance are the Brigands led by Ron Marston, but should the players decide to search for the barn once they have gained knowledge of it, they will rather quickly find it as there are not many barns in the direct vicinity of the estate grounds.

The Secret Barn Entrance becomes unavailable after it is compromised, as the guards seal it off completely.